**W9-BJE-820**

Her hand seemed to move of its own volition. She slapped him full across the face and then stared up at him in horror.

He put his hands on either side of her face and, pulling her towards him, he kissed her full on the mouth. Abigail began to struggle but he held her close. That clever sensuous mouth moved against her own, softening from a punishing kiss into a long, languorous one. The surge of emotion, of passion, that gripped her stopped her struggles. Her hands, which had been beating on his shoulders, stole up round his neck instead. The military band outside was playing a waltz, the library smelt of leather, beeswax, and roses. He smelt of cologne and soap.

He drew back a little and looked down at her anxiously, remembering how terrified she had been of Harry's love-making. "I am sorry," he began, but she gazed up at him with a drowned look and drew his mouth down to hers. . . .

By Marion Chesney
*Published by Fawcett Books:*

# THE DECEPTION

## Marion Chesney

FAWCETT CREST • NEW YORK

A Fawcett Crest Book
Published by Ballantine Books
Copyright © 1996 by Marion Chesney

http://www.randomhouse.com

Library of Congress Catalog Card Number: 96-90981

ISBN 0-449-22559-3

This edition published by arrangement with St. Martin's Press, Inc.

Manufactured in the United States of America

First Ballantine Books Edition: May 1997

10   9   8   7   6   5   4   3   2   1

*This series is dedicated to*
*Rosemary Barradell, with love*

# Chapter One

*Destructive, damnable, deceitful woman!*
—THOMAS OTWAY

THE BEVERLEY TWINS were very alike in appearance, but Rachel was softer in nature than Abigail. Sometimes Abigail thought she was made of steel compared to her sisters. Jessica had proved to be a squeamish weakling. Mannerling was what mattered.

The six Beverley sisters and their parents had lost their home, Mannerling, due to Sir William Beverley's debts. They had moved to modest Brookfield House some miles away. The two elder girls, Isabella and Jessica, who, Abigail believed, had almost had Mannerling in their grasp through marriage, had thrown away all for love. Jessica had actually been engaged to the son of the present owners, Mr. and Mrs. Devers, but had turned him down because, she said, he had assaulted her. In all her virginal innocence, Abigail believed that all Harry Devers had done was to kiss her sister too warmly, not knowing he had nearly raped her. Such matters were not discussed in a genteel home. The youngest, Lizzie, knew something really dreadful had happened, but time had moved on and gradually the myth that Jessica had behaved too *missishly* became more and more to be believed by Abigail and her twin, Rachel, who was often easily swayed by her.

There was no doubt that Mannerling exerted a

powerful influence over all who lived there. It was a well-known fact that Harry Devers wanted the place for himself, and if he married would expect his parents to live elsewhere. It was admittedly a graceful mansion with two wings springing out from a central block and a porticoed entrance. The double staircase and the painted ceiling were accounted to be among the finest in the country.

After Jessica's wedding to "a mere professor," Abigail found that she was once more possessed by all the longing for her old home.

"I would not have behaved like Jessica," she said to Rachel for what seemed to her twin like the umpteenth time. Rachel looked at her doubtfully. The twins were dressed alike in simple muslin gowns, both had fair hair and large blue eyes, but Abigail's eyes always gazed out at the world with confident certainty while Rachel's held a bewildered innocence. "I have just learned Harry Devers is due home on leave quite soon," she added.

"How did you come by such intelligence?" asked Rachel curiously. "Miss Trumble would never tell us even if she knew." Miss Trumble was their governess.

"Mary Stoddart—I mean, Mary Judd. She said it to taunt me."

Mary Stoddart was the vicar's daughter, who had been temporarily mistress of Mannerling when she had married one of the owners, a Mr. Judd. She was now a widow, her husband having hanged himself when he realized he was about to lose Mannerling because of his gambling debts. Debt had also been the curse of the girls' father, Sir William, who had died of typhoid not long after gambling away their home.

"Harry Devers will not come near us, nor will his parents let him."

"But surely we could contrive a way to come across him," said Abigail. "He will go out riding, and perhaps we could be walking past at the time."

From her window upstairs, Miss Trumble looked down and saw the twins walking in the garden. She was struck afresh every time she saw them at how alike they looked. She had suggested that they might choose different gowns and different colours, but the twins were inseparable and preferred to dress alike. They were both remarkably pretty, thought Miss Trumble, and should be going to balls and parties.

She frowned. Lady Beverley was miserly and kept complaining that there was not enough money to take them about. But the governess had learned from Barry Wort, the odd man, to whom Isabella, the eldest, frequently wrote, that Isabella's husband, Lord Fitzpatrick, sent sums of money, as did Jessica's husband, Professor Sommerville. She made her way downstairs with a warm shawl wrapped about her shoulders against the autumn chill, wondering how it was that neither of the twins ever appeared to feel the cold, even dressed as they were that morning in filmy muslin. She had suspended their lessons because Lizzie, the youngest, was ill with a bad cold, and her elder sisters were becoming increasingly rebellious at the idea of lessons in the schoolroom. The twins were aged nineteen, the next in line, Belinda, was eighteen, and Lizzie was seventeen.

As she walked out into the garden, the twins saw her and hurried away. She stood frowning, watching them go, wondering if they were plotting anything. She was constantly worried that what she privately dubbed as "the Mannerling madness" would surface in one of them again. Surely not. With Mr. and Mrs. Devers still the owners of Mannerling and with their son having shown himself to be a lecher and a lout, there could surely be no danger any more.

She went round the back of the house to find Barry, the odd man, whom she often used as a confidant, thinking him the most sensible member of the household.

Barry was feeding the hens, who clucked around his feet. He was a square, stocky man, a former soldier, of a placid disposition. Miss Trumble hailed him and Barry looked up with a smile as she came across the garden towards him.

He wondered again about the mystery that surrounded Miss Trumble. She was old, in her sixties, with a wrinkled face and fine brown eyes. But she moved with grace and had a certain aristocratic air. She never discussed her previous employers, talked about her family, or explained how it was that she always seemed to have a comfortable amount of money which did not, thought Barry, come from her wages which, he knew, Lady Beverley often "forgot" to pay.

"I saw the twins walking in the garden," said Miss Trumble, "and went to join them but they scurried off. I hope they are not plotting anything. Probably they were frightened that I would drag them up to the schoolroom for more lessons."

Barry put the now empty wooden bowl which had contained the food for the hens down on the ground. "I hear Harry Devers is due home on leave soon."

"Oh, no! Make sure the girls do not learn of that! But even if they did, surely they cannot still harbour ambitions in that direction. The man is dangerous!"

"Perhaps they do not know that, miss."

"No, virginity makes all seem innocent."

Barry wondered what had happened in Miss Trumble's life to remove her innocence.

"But to get to my immediate problem," said the governess. "How do I get Lady Beverley to loosen the purse-strings so that my girls can have new gowns and go to balls and assemblies?"

"I cannot think, miss. Reckon my lady will claim poverty as usual."

"There is a grand ball in the offing at Lady Evans's, you know, at Hursley Park on the other side of Hedgefield. The invitations have not yet been sent out. I would like to secure invitations for the girls. How are they going to find husbands kept mewed up here? I feel sure if I spoke to Lady Evans, she would oblige me."

"Beg pardon, miss, but why would such a grand lady as Lady Evans feel she had to oblige a governess?"

"I think she is probably good-hearted and not at all high in the instep," said Miss Trumble, turning away.

She went into the house by the kitchen door. Josiah, the one-legged cook, was scowling furiously at some old, yellowed bits of parchment.

His face cleared when he saw Miss Trumble. "My reading don't be what it should be," said the cook. "Here is a recipe for Batalia pie. Would you be so good as to read it out for me? I have a good memory and once I hear something, I never forget it."

Miss Trumble picked up a piece of parchment and studied the old-fashioned writing. It said:

*Take four tame Pigeons and Truss them to bake, and take four Ox Pallets well boyled and blaunched, and cut it in little peeces, take six Lamb-stones, and as many good sweet Breads of Veale cut in halfs*

*and parboyld, and twenty Cockscombs boyled and
blanched and the bottoms of four Artichokes, and a
Pint of Oysters parboyld and bearded, and the
Marrow of three bones, so season all with Mace,
Nutmeg, and Salt, so put your meat in a fine Coffin
of fine Past proportionable to your quantity of meat,
put half a pound of Butter upon your meat, put a
little water in the Pye, before it be set in the Oven,
let it stand in the Oven an hour and a half, then
take it out, pour out the butter at the top of the Pye,
and put it in a leer of Gravy, Butter, and Lemons
and serve it up.*

"What are lamb-stones, miss?"

"Kidneys."

"I'd best leave them out. The pigeons are our own,
but I don't reckon my lady will allow me to buy
kidneys."

Miss Trumble fished in her reticule and pulled out
some silver. "Here, Josiah, buy your kidneys and
take the horse into Hedgefield."

"My lady won't like a servant using the horse."

"She will not know the purpose. I shall merely say
I told you to exercise the animal."

Miss Trumble sat down at the scrubbed kitchen
table after the cook had left to go on his errand. The
kitchen was warm and scented by the bunches of
dried herbs hanging from the ceiling and from the
smell of biscuits, recently baked in the brick-built
oven. Miss Trumble loved to watch Josiah bake. He
would bake the bread first, when the oven was
hottest, then small bread, buns, cakes, and biscuits.
In the last of the heat, when all the baking was finished, feathers and down for pillows were dried and
fluffed, and rose petals and herbs dried for pot-pourri

and the store cupboard. It took great experience and intuition to regulate the heat.

Miss Trumble knew that it was not very ladylike in her to favour the kitchen over all other rooms in the house, and yet there was a simple reason for her liking—it was the only warm room in the house.

That thought made her cudgel her brains about how to deal with Lady Beverley's parsimony. Then her face cleared. She had hit on a plan. Hitching her stole about her shoulders with an unconscious grace, she went to the parlour, where she knew she would find Lady Beverley brooding over the household accounts.

"My lady?"

Lady Beverley turned round, a wary look in her eyes when she saw the governess. She was all too aware that she had not paid Miss Trumble any wages the last quarter-day.

"Miss Trumble?"

"My lady, I hear Lady Evans is to give a ball. It would be exceeding good if the girls were invited."

Lady Beverley's face took on a petulant look. "I have not the funds for the necessary fripperies they will demand."

"As to that, I had the economy of this household in mind, my lady."

"Indeed! How so?"

"The girls are young and healthy and eat a great deal. If they go on in seclusion, you will have four spinsters on your hands, four spinsters to feed and clothe until the end of your days. On the other hand, were they to find husbands, *rich* husbands, then not only would they cease to be a burden on the household expense, but perhaps their husbands could contribute to the costs."

There was a sudden gleam in Lady Beverley's eyes. Then she said, "But I do not know Lady Evans. She is but lately moved into the neighbourhood and has not sent cards, nor have I called."

"Perhaps you would be so good as to leave the matter in my hands?"

"You! What can you do?"

"Just leave it to me," said Miss Trumble, edging to the door.

When she had gone, Lady Beverley gave a contemptuous sniff. Miss Trumble would meet with a set-down if she dared to call on Lady Evans, and that would do her no harm at all. The governess was often a trifle too uppity for her position.

The sun was shining but it was another cold day and the frost was only just melting from the grass. Miss Trumble heard cries from the garden and looked out. Abigail, Rachel, Belinda, and Lizzie were playing at battledore and shuttlecock. As usual, Abigail was the most energetic of all, flying here and there, her long fair hair glinting in the sunshine, her face flushed.

Miss Trumble stifled a little sigh. It was a hard world for women. Had Abigail been a man, then all that energy could have been channelled into more useful purposes. She could have been a soldier, run estates, managed a business. But because she was a mere girl, all ambition was directed towards getting a husband. No wonder the bright Beverley girls had tried so hard to get their old home back. Such determined ambition in a man would have been commended, whereas in the Beverleys, it was considered vulgar.

She turned and went upstairs to change into one

of her best gowns. When Josiah returned, the horse would need to be hitched to the carriage to take her to Hursley Park.

After the game was over, Lizzie and Belinda rushed indoors, not being impervious to the cold like the twins. In Belinda's room, they tipped out twigs and branches on the floor in front of the fireplace that they had collected in their aprons before the game and piled up on the grass. "Let's build up the fire," said Belinda, shivering.

"Barry would find us a few logs if we asked him," said Lizzie, piling the twigs and broken branches in the fireplace.

"We will need to wait until Mama lies down for her nap," said Belinda, striking the tinder-box and sending a small fountain of sparks down onto the branches. "What think you of Rachel and Abigail these days?"

"What do you mean?"

"They are excluding us from some plot. They always have their heads together and when we approach they fall silent."

"I hope it is nothing to do with Mannerling," said Lizzie anxiously. "Abigail did say she thought Jessica had been over-missish, but I think Harry Devers is, like Byron, 'mad, bad, and dangerous to know.' "

"And he can't even write poetry," said Belinda with a giggle. "It can't be anything to do with Harry Devers. We will never see him again." She grew suddenly serious. "I sometimes think we will never see *anyone* again. We no longer even go on calls to the squire. Church on a Sunday is the big event of our week, and being preached to by Mary's father is not very soul-lifting. If only something would happen."

Lizzie said, "I spoke of this to Barry and he said

that our Miss Trumble would be bound to make something happen."

"Miss Trumble is a lady of many surprises," said Belinda, "but hardly of a social status to be able to do anything for us."

Lady Evans was a rather grim-looking dowager with a lined face under a formidable cap. She looked at her butler in amazement and then down at the card he had presented to her. "I do not know a Miss Trumble."

"I believe a Miss Trumble to be a governess to the Beverley girls at Brookfield House."

Lady Evans gave a click of impatience. "What can she want? My daughters are married. I have no need of a governess."

"I have heard, my lady, in Hedgefield, that this Miss Trumble does a certain amount of work among the poor."

Lady Evans's face cleared. "Then she has no doubt come to see if we have old clothes or money for a donation. It would be churlish not to see her. Send her up."

While she waited, Lady Evans wondered whether to ask her lady's-maid to look out some clothes or to present this Miss Trumble with a small donation. Perhaps it would be best to wait to see what was required.

"Miss Trumble," intoned the butler, holding open the door of the drawing-room.

Lady Evans swung round. "Ah, Miss . . ."

Her voice died away as Miss Trumble put a finger to her lips.

"That will be all," said Lady Evans faintly. The butler bowed and withdrew. "Letitia," said Lady

Evans. "By all that's holy, how have you come to this pass? And why are you calling yourself Trumble?"

"I will tell you but it must be our secret," said Miss Trumble. She sat down gracefully by the fire and began to talk. Lady Evans listened, wide-eyed. When Miss Trumble had finished, she said, "Your secret is safe with me, but why you should lead such an uncomfortable and degrading life schooling a parcel of misses is beyond me. Can I help in any way?"

"Yes, indeed, and that is why I am come. First I must tell you about the Beverley obsession with Mannerling, an obsession I must admit of which, I hope, they have all been cured. You have no doubt heard from local gossip how they were vastly rich and proud and lived at Mannerling. They tried to reclaim it through marriage, but fortunately the two elder girls made suitable marriages for love. Their last attempt nearly ended in disaster, for Harry Devers was the target. But no doubt you have heard that scandal."

"Yes, I did. And I must admit I took against these Beverley girls. Such blatant ambition is so crude."

"And yet such ambition would not be considered crude in a man. Do you remember young Charlie Anderson? He was about to lose his home and estates and was at his wit's end. He married a sugar heiress, a blowsy common girl from the West Indies. How clever of him, everyone said. What sterling behaviour!"

Lady Evans gave a reluctant laugh.

"And my girls are as good as they are beautiful," pursued Miss Trumble. "Lady Beverley, perhaps because of such misfortunes, has become somewhat of a miser, and my ladies do not go anywhere. To

11

that end I am come to beg you to send them invitations to your ball."

"I will do this for you, Letitia. I am now curious to see them. I will have a fair number of eligible men at the ball, but what hope have you when, as I gather, they have no dowries? It is very odd that the two married for love because, as you know, that usually only happens in books. Any man's family will quickly find out all about the Beverleys and dissuade him if he shows any sign of taking an interest. But we will see. We were talking of young Harry Devers. Do you know he is expected home on leave?"

Miss Trumble's heart gave a lurch. Barry had told her that but it hadn't really seemed anything to worry about. Now she had a sudden vivid picture of the twins' fleeing at her approach. But she said, "I doubt very much if we will see anything of him. He will not be at your ball, I hope?"

"No, he will not. Mrs. Devers called. She kept assuring me he was a sweet boy and a completely reformed character."

"That one will never reform," said Miss Trumble with a shudder.

Lady Evans rang the bell. "You must take tea, Letitia, and we will talk about the old days. So few of us left!"

Barry lounged outside, talking to one of the grooms, but privately wondering what was keeping Miss Trumble so long. He had thought it a bit forward of her to approach Lady Evans on the matter of invitations to the ball and had expected her to emerge from the house after only a few moments. But the sun sank lower in the sky, burning red through the skeletal branches of the trees bordering the drive, and still Miss Trumble did not appear.

It was a full hour later and he had already lit the carriage lamps when Miss Trumble emerged.

"How did it go?" asked Barry.

"Very successful," said Miss Trumble, drawing the carriage rug up over her legs.

"You just asked, just like that?"

"Just like that," said Miss Trumble calmly. "Lady Evans is a friend of one of my previous employers and was always kind to me."

"Which employer was that, miss?"

"Barry, would you be so good as to stop at the coal merchant's in Hedgefield? I have a desire to order a quantity of coal."

"Coal is expensive, miss."

"Indeed it is, which is why Lady Beverley never has enough. We will let her assume it came from some mysterious benefactor."

"And I reckon you'd consider it impertinent were I to ask you where you found the money for such a luxury?"

"Very impertinent. Drive on."


The Beverleys were all in the parlour the following afternoon when Barry appeared carrying a scuttleful of coal. He proceeded to pile coal on the meagre fire.

"What are you doing?" demanded Lady Beverley. "You are putting a month's coal ration on that fire."

"A ton of coal arrived this morning as a present from an unknown benefactor," said Barry.

"Oh, how nice!" Lady Beverley looked delighted at this unexpected largess for which she did not have to pay.

"Dear me," said Miss Trumble, putting down a piece of sewing she had been working on, "I would have thought you might have considered it a trifle humiliating, my lady."

"How so?"

"As the girls go nowhere socially and have no admirers, the gift was obviously prompted by charity."

"Charity!" Abigail looked shocked.

"Well, you know how it is." Miss Trumble bent her head over her sewing again. "Shopkeepers will gossip, and to their betters, too. It is well known that this household buys the cheapest of everything—the cheapest cuts of meat, tallow candles, things like that. So it has got about how very poor we are."

"We are not poor!" Lady Beverley looked outraged. "Merely thrifty." She fumbled for her smelling salts.

"Of course, my lady," murmured Miss Trumble.

Barry suppressed a smile as he left the room.

A few moments later, he popped his head round the door. "Footman coming up the drive, my lady."

"Mannerling!" cried Abigail. "It is an invitation to Mannerling."

Miss Trumble walked to the window and looked out. "It is not the Mannerling livery," she said quietly. Then she turned and looked thoughtfully at Abigail, who blushed a miserable red, suddenly aware that she had betrayed herself to this sharp-eyed governess.

Now there's going to be trouble, thought Rachel, feeling suddenly guilty and wishing she had never encouraged Abigail to talk about Harry Devers.

The maid, Betty, came in, dropped a curtsy, and handed Lady Beverley a pile of invitations. "Dear me," said Lady Beverley, "Lady Evans has invited us all to a ball at Hursley Park next month at the full moon. How extraordinary! There is even an invitation for Miss Trumble as well. How odd to invite a mere servant."

"Lady Evans was a friend of one of my previous employers," said Miss Trumble quietly. "I took the liberty of calling on her yesterday. If you but remember, my lady. I told you I was going. The girls are in need of new ball gowns. Of course, if they go in their old ones, perhaps someone else in the neighbourhood will decide to honour us with some more charity."

"That is enough," said Lady Beverley sharply. "My girls shall have the best. Gowns must be ordered for them, and from London, too."

The next couple of days were a bustle of activity. Their measurements had to be carefully made and dummies of the girls prepared in wood by the local carpenter. Where Miss Trumble had managed to secure all the latest fashion magazines from was a mystery, but the girls were too happy and excited to ask. Fashions were chosen, and then Barry had to load up the dummies, complete with a letter of instructions to take to the mail coach, where they would be hurtled up to the dressmaker in London.

In all the excitement, Abigail had hoped that Miss Trumble had forgotten that cry of "Mannerling," but no sooner had Barry rumbled off in the little open carriage with the wooden dummies lurching crazily in the back that Miss Trumble said, "Abigail, Rachel. A word, if you please."

Both looked to their mother, hoping she would delay them, but Lady Beverley was bent over the household accounts again, her lips moving soundlessly.

Reluctantly they followed their governess out of the room. "My room, I think," said Miss Trumble, leading the way upstairs. The room was neat and clean, with a large fire blazing in the hearth. "Draw up chairs by the fire," commanded Miss Trumble. When the girls were seated, she said, "I was disturbed at your eagerness, Abigail, to believe that footman was from Mannerling. You ought not to have been considering any invitation from Mannerling with anything other than dread. You are not to see or go near Harry Devers again . . . either of you."

Abigail tossed her fair curls. "Who are you to command us as to who we should see or not see? That is for Mama to say."

Miss Trumble sighed. "Which means you still harbour ambitions in that direction, you silly girls. Jessica was assaulted and arrived here with her gown ripped. What on earth do you think happened to her? Too warm a kiss? This craziness must cease."

Rachel flashed a guilty look at her twin and mumbled, "We thought perhaps Jessica had been a trifle missish."

"Missish! Your sister was brutally assaulted and frightened out of her wits."

The twins hung their heads.

"Let me hear no more of your nonsense," said Miss Trumble severely. "You must look your prettiest for this ball. There will be eligible men there. If you behave well, then other invitations will be forthcoming. Now, off with you!"

The twins went out. Each usually knew what the other was thinking and so, by a sort of unspoken agreement, they went to Abigail's room. Abigail sat down wearily on the edge of the bed. "She did make me feel the most utter fool."

"I feel she spoke nothing but the truth about Harry and Jessica," said Rachel. "I remember now that Jessica's gown was ripped, but what happened was evidently so awful that no one would tell us about it and I had forgotten about the state Jessica arrived home in that day."

"Perhaps if it stays dry tomorrow," said Abigail, "we will walk over to Mannerling for one last look. I feel if I go and say goodbye, then my brain won't trick me any more."

"We will not be allowed to go out walking alone," said Rachel.

"We will take pails and say we are going to pick blackberries. Then we can leave the pails in the nearest hedge and make our way."

Miss Trumble was so sure that she had knocked sense into their heads that she did not worry about anything when she saw the twins setting out with pails to collect blackberries. She would have been worried had she known that Lizzie and Belinda had offered to go with them and had been rudely told that their company was not wanted.

After hiding their pails in the hedgerow and resolving to pick at least some blackberries before they returned home, Rachel and Abigail made their way towards Mannerling, under a clear, cold blue sky, the iron rings on their pattens clattering on the frost-hard road. Birds piped cold little dismal cries from the hedgerows, which gleamed red with hips and haws. There was a scent of decay in the air.

When they reached the great gates of Mannerling, they both gazed hungrily through the iron bars.

The gardens had been laid out in the last century by Capability Brown. He had earned the nickname Capability because of the noble simplicity of his vision in remodelling great parks. In fact, his boast was that he could not go to Ireland because he had not yet finished refashioning England. The gardens at Mannerling contained all the hallmarks of Brown's landscaping. Great sweeps of greensward, relieved by clumps of trees, extended right up to the house itself and sloped down to a level sheet of water created from diminutive streams. A belt of trees encircled the whole park, breaking in places to open up vistas onto the surrounding country. Humphry Repton, Brown's successor, had added the long line of trees on either side of the drive, the rose garden, the kitchen garden, and the terraces.

The sound of a carriage made the twins turn round in alarm. It was shameful to be discovered thus in their old gowns. The carriage stopped and Mrs. Devers looked out. "Pray join me, ladies," she called as the footman jumped down from the back-strap to let down the carriage steps. "We will take a dish of tea."

The normally haughty Mrs. Devers's impulse was prompted because she felt "poor Harry" was still in deep disgrace because of that "little misunderstanding" over Jessica Beverley. Therefore it followed that if she became on good terms with the Beverley family, people would discount that story about Harry.

Rachel and Abigail shared the same thought as they climbed into the carriage. How furious Miss Trumble would be if she could see them now.

Once inside Mannerling, Abigail gazed about her with something close to despair. So does a woman feel when she thinks the obsession she has suffered for some man has finally left her, only to see him again and find the obsession is as strong as ever. Every room seemed to call to her, "I belong to you."

"I think this place is haunted," said Mrs. Devers as she led the way into the drawing-room.

"By Mr. Judd?" asked Rachel.

"No, I think it takes people's souls. I would have persuaded Mr. Devers to sell it, but of course Harry would not hear of it. He loves this place."

She rang the bell and asked for tea to be served. Soon the tea-kettle was bubbling on its tall three-legged stand. Japanned trays swirling with patterns of blush roses were carried in, laden with biscuits. Then there was the cake basket they remembered, and wondered why their mother had not taken it with her. It had "barley-sugar" handles and pierced sides. The rosewood tea caddy and silver tea-strainer, the little silver cream jug, all stood on fragile tables among the cups and saucers of so thin and fine a china as to be almost transparent.

"I believe Lady Evans over at Hursley Park is to give a ball," said Mrs. Devers.

"Yes, we are invited to go," said Abigail proudly.

"Really! I have no doubt our invitations will be arriving shortly. I apprised Lady Evans of the intelligence that Harry is shortly due home on leave. This terrible war. Will it never end?"

The twins said nothing. The lecture from Miss Trumble still rang in their ears.

"Of course," went on Mrs. Devers hurriedly and without her usual stately calm, "Harry did behave so badly towards your sister and it did get about. But he was always such a *wild* boy. Young men are so headstrong, and he was so terribly much in love with your sister that he got quite *carried away*. He is such a *romantic* fellow and he knew he was losing Jessica's affections to his cousin, Robert Sommerville, and he lost his head. He has been so dreadfully punished for his folly and has become so *changed*, so quiet and gentlemanly, you would not recognize him at all."

"Perhaps he will be at Lady Evans's ball," suggested Abigail.

Mrs. Devers busied herself with the tea-kettle. "Well, as to that," she said with an awkward laugh, "Lady Evans is so very *old*, don't you know, and the old are so intolerant of foibles in the young, quite as if they had never been young themselves."

Miss Trumble, thought Abigail, would no doubt wonder acidly whether Lady Evans had assaulted anyone in *her* youth.

Rachel changed the subject and chatted about the dresses they were having made for the ball at one of London's leading dressmaker's. Mrs. Devers then turned the conversation to London, saying she had been there recently, and began talking of plays and operas she had seen.

The twins suddenly realized that time was passing, and if they did not hurry, Barry would be sent out looking for them. They rose to their feet to make their goodbyes.

"But you must not walk," Mrs. Devers exclaimed. "I will send you home in the carriage."

Rachel opened her mouth to say hurriedly that they would enjoy the walk home and heard, to her horror, Abigail accepting the offer. She did not say anything until they were in the carriage and bowling down the drive.

"Are you run mad?" she demanded angrily. "What will happen when Miss Trumble sees us arriving in the Mannerling carriage?"

"She won't," said Abigail. "We'll tell the coachman to stop where we left the pails and walk from there."

Rachel heaved a sigh of relief.

* * *

Miss Trumble met them as they came in, swinging their empty pails. "No blackberries?" she asked.

"Not a one," said Abigail cheerfully. "We were playing at swinging our pails and we upset them all over the road."

"Where was that?"

"Beyond the entrance to Currie's farm, where that thick hedgerow is," said Abigail.

After dinner, Miss Trumble took a lantern and walked along the road until she reached the hedgerow by Currie's farm. She held the lantern high. Frost sparkled like marcasite on the road, but of spilled blackberries there was not any sign at all.

She walked slowly back. Should she accuse them of lying? Where had they really been? But if she accused them, that might make them more secretive than ever. She would wait and watch.


The fine weather broke and the rain came down in floods, turning the roads about Brookfield House to rivers of mud. The girls began to fret. The roads were impassable. Their dresses would never arrive in time, and how could they get to the ball anyway in such weather? Even Miss Trumble began to lose hope and suggested they look out their old gowns so that she might reshape them.

But the rain ceased as suddenly as it had come, followed by an unseasonably warm drying wind from the south. The dresses duly arrived and everything was set fair for the ball.

Miss Trumble received a note from Lady Evans. In it Lady Evans had listed the eligibles who were to attend the ball and said, "Lord Burfield is the prize. He is vastly rich and vastly handsome. But he is in his early thirties and no girl has caught his eye yet. I wonder why?"

I wonder, too, thought Miss Trumble. He might prove to be another Harry Devers!

## Chapter Two

*O, Love's but a dance,*
*Where Time plays the fiddle!*
*See the couples advance,—*
*O, Love's but a dance!*
*A whisper, a glance,—*
*"Shall we twirl down the middle?"*
*O, Love's but a dance,*
*Where Time plays the fiddle!*
                    —HENRY AUSTIN DOBSON

LORD BURFIELD WOULD have not been in the least surprised had he learned that he was the talk of every family that was to attend the ball. He was used to being the centre of attention. As a child, he had been doted on by his parents—a most unusual state of affairs in the Regency, where children were expected to stay out of sight, watched over by governesses or tutors. But he had been a rosy-cheeked cherub with a mop of golden curls, and the pet of the servants as well.

He had left the comfort of his home at the age of eighteen to join the army. His father, the Earl of Drezby, had cried fond and proud tears at the sight of his golden-haired boy in his hussar uniform. It was a tradition in England that the aristocracy went into the army and the gentry to the navy, and neither the earl nor the countess expected army life to change their sweet-natured scholarly son in the slightest. Rupert, Lord Burfield, had ridden off to fight the French and ended up in the misery of the Duke of York's disastrous campaign in the Low Countries. The countryside was in the grip of ferocious frosts, and it was, wrongly, assumed that the French would keep to their quarters until the hard winter was over. But the French came speeding down the frozen canals, defeated the Dutch, seized all their ports, and sent the exhausted redcoats staggering towards Hanover, into a new hell of cold and wretchedness. "I shall not feel this as a severe blow," the Duke of York wrote to his royal father, but the British public viewed it differently and chanted in the streets:

> *The noble Duke of York*
> *He had ten thousand men,*
> *He marched them up to the top of the hill,*
> *And he marched them down again.*

As one of the unhappy ten thousand who had done the marching, Lord Burfield prayed to be home as soon as possible, but he was kept an extra six weeks on the banks of the Waal by the French, sleeping in his clothes and turning out once or twice a night. From across the river, the French shouted insults. Nor was his mood helped by the contempt he had for his fellow officers. There was a scandalous traffic in field offices by army brokers who made an officer out of anyone who could pay. And the rank and file were a disgrace. The Duke of Wellington was to describe them as "the off-scouring of the nation, who could be purchased at a cheap rate by the crimps—criminals, decrepit old men, raw boys, the half-witted, the feeble-minded, even downright lunatics."

The wagon-train was named The Newgate Blues, after London's most notorious prison.

Lord Burfield, who had endured a rigorous training at a military academy before gaining his captaincy, was appalled at the degradation he saw all around him. His golden curls were full of lice, so he shaved his head and wore a wig. When they finally marched towards the river Ems and then to Bremen and the Weser, Lord Burfield watched men break ranks to loot. The weather was so cruel that many of the men stumbled and fell, to add their bodies to the piles of already frozen bodies by the roadsides.

The innocence left Lord Burfield's blue eyes, and his face thinned and hardened. He was sickened by the sights of war and felt he had aged years. But he did not leave the army. Instead, he applied his wits to studying more war strategy, determined to be the best officer he could find it within himself to be. After the Low Countries, under the command of Colonel Arthur Wesley, later to become the Duke of Wellington, he sailed to India, where he fought well and served the first man in the army he had found to admire.

After the Indian campaigns he returned to London on leave, to enjoy his first Season. He had become a tall man, just over six feet in height, with sun-bleached hair cut in a Brutus crop and a handsome tanned face with a firm square chin below a passionate and sensitive mouth. He was rich and he was handsome, and the ladies flocked to his side. But although he enjoyed a few light affairs with bored married ladies, he found the frivolities of the London Season shallow and empty. He returned to the army and served five more years, until he inherited his great-uncle's house and estates. He sold out and settled down to the life of a landowner. He was thirty-three and reluctantly decided that he should find a bride. He was staying with Lady Evans, a friend of his parents'.

He was sitting taking tea with his hostess in her drawing-room at Hursley Park a week before the ball when he said to her, half-jokingly, that he had a mind to marry.

"And who is the lucky girl?" asked Lady Evans, her great starched cap casting a shadow over her face as she leaned forward to pour more tea.

"There isn't one," he said. "But there should be plenty of young misses at this ball of yours. One has only to drop the handkerchief."

"For one of them to snatch it up? How arrogant you sound!"

"I suppose I do."

"I trust you are contemplating courting some lady and getting to know her and her family first?"

"I find the idea of a courtship boring. I cannot talk of serious matters. I must compliment and flirt, she must simper and sigh, her parents will assess the amount of my fortune and give their blessing."

"What if you should fall in love with a lady who has no fortune?"

"I doubt if that will ever happen. I would assume any penniless miss who wanted me would have her eye on my moneybags. And talking of mercenary misses, what is all this fascinating gossip about the beautiful Beverley sisters?"

"What have you heard?"

He stretched out his long legs and watched the reflection of the flames burning among the apple logs in the hearth shining on his Hessian boots. "It was at dinner the other night. Young Mr. Harris said they would never find husbands with their reputations. I was fascinated by the vision of sinful young girls. But evidently their sin is only in their lust for their old home and in their plotting and scheming to get it back.

"It all sounded such a Gothic tale. One owner committed suicide, the Beverley father ruined and dying of typhoid, and yet when I asked about the two elder girls who are married, I learned to my surprise that they married exceptionally well, and all for unfashionable love, too. Is this Mannerling such an enchanted house?"

"I have not called there yet, so I do not know. If you heard all that gossip, you no doubt heard about the Deverses' son, Harry, a rake and libertine and half mad?"

He nodded.

"That is the reason I decided not to call. There certainly seems to be something weird about Mannerling, for the hedonistic Harry is said to be obsessed with the place."

"In any case, you will have a chance to meet the Beverly girls, the four remaining ones, that is. I have invited them all to my ball."

"Indeed! And you such a high stickler."

"I have my reasons, which are private."

"I become more intrigued by the moment. Perhaps if the weather holds fine, I will ride over tomorrow and have a look at this Mannerling."

"Do not call!" exclaimed Lady Evans. " 'Twould be most awkward, considering the Deverses are not invited here."

"Be reassured. I shall simply look."

Rachel had a bad cold and lay in bed with a handkerchief to her little red nose, moaning that if she did not get better soon, she would not be able to go to the ball. Miss Trumble was nursing her and chiding her in a rallying voice to concentrate on getting well and to forget about the ball. Abigail left her twin's bedroom and put a warm cloak over her gown and a sturdy pair of half-boots on her feet, a felt hat on her fair curls, and set out for a walk. She had not told anyone she was going, only meaning to walk a little way along the road. But the day was crisp and clear and somehow she found she was taking the road to Mannerling. A cow leaned over a fence, its breath steaming in the cold air. She patted its nose absentmindedly. Now that all the excitement of having a brand-new ball gown in the very latest fashion had begun to ebb, she felt slightly lost, as one does when a burning ambition has fled. Mannerling was gone. Despite Mrs. Devers's remarks about her son being a reformed character, Abigail did not believe it. In romantic novels, the hero was always being reformed by the "love of a good woman." But the sensible Miss Trumble had forcibly pointed out that this did not happen in real life. Abigail gave a little sigh. Perhaps she should concentrate her mind on looking as pretty as possible at the ball, and try to find a husband. What would it be like to be in love? she mused as she walked steadily along the rutted road. All her young thoughts had been so taken up with Mannerling that she had never had any space in her head for other dreams. A house of her own would be fine, and perhaps children. She tried to conjure up a vision of a husband, but he remained shadowy.

She came to the gates of Mannerling and put her gloved hands on the iron bars, like someone in prison, and stared hungrily down the drive.

And that is how Lord Burfield first saw her. So

intent was Abigail in staring at her old home that she did not hear the approach of the horseman.

Lord Burfield reined in his horse and swung down from the saddle and stood looking at the slim figure of Abigail, her hands clutching the gates of Mannerling.

He took her for an upper servant, for he knew no lady went out walking unaccompanied. Or perhaps, he thought, she was the lodge-keeper's daughter. Suddenly, as if aware of his gaze, she swung round and gazed full up into his face. He caught his breath. It was an enchanting little face with thick lashes framing eyes as blue as his own. He swept off his hat and made a low bow.

Abigail gave a tentative smile and began to back away down the road.

"It is a fine day, miss," ventured Lord Burfield.

She nodded, turned, and began to walk hurriedly away. It was then he noticed the richness of her fur-lined cloak.

"Are you by any chance," he called after her, "one of the Misses Beverley?"

She turned round again and walked back towards him, her eyes wary. "Yes, sir."

"Then we will meet at the ball. I am a guest of Lady Evans. My name is Burfield."

"Lord Burfield?" asked Abigail, assuming that if he were a plain mister he would have said so. She dropped a curtsy. "I am Miss Abigail Beverley."

"I am delighted to make your acquaintance. May I ask why it is that you are out walking without a maid or footman to accompany you?"

Her face flamed and she began to stammer, "I–I k–know it is wrong of m–me. You will not tell? I often go walking on my own. My twin is ill with the cold. Sometimes I feel so 'cabin'd cribb'd, confin'd.' "

He raised his eyebrows. It was unusual to come across any young miss who quoted Shakespeare. He smiled. "And how is it you come to be 'bound in to saucy doubts and fears'?"

She sighed. "I was restless."

"So, Miss Abigail, you stand outside the gates of your old home like a peri outside the gates of Paradise."

She blushed again. "You know of us?"

"Gossip moves freely in the country. Come, I will accompany you a little way." He glanced through the gates. "A fine house, but only a house. I came to view the haunted mansion."

"Haunted?"

"It seems to exercise a powerful influence on all who have anything to do with the place." Leading his horse, he fell into step beside her.

"You must not walk all the way home with me," said Abigail anxiously. "For I am not supposed to be out on my own and must enter quietly from the back."

"I promise to disappear as soon as your home comes in sight."

They walked on. He gave a little shiver. "I am always glad when summer is with us again. Ever since my days in India, I feel the cold more than any Englishman should."

Abigail looked up at the tall figure shyly. "You were in India?"

"Yes, under the command of Colonel Wesley, although, now I remember, the family name was changed to Wellesley while our Iron Duke was still in India."

Abigail forgot her shyness. "Were you at the siege of Seringapatam?" she asked eagerly.

"Yes, Miss Abigail."

"Oh, do tell me about it. It must have been monstrous exciting to fight the Tiger of Mysore."

Tippu Sultan, the Tiger of Mysore, had been in league with the French. Lord Burfield was surprised this young miss had even heard of the siege. "I believe the ladies do not like stories of war."

"But I do. For you were actually there!"

And so he began to tell her while his mind wandered back to the Indian days. He remembered the ferocious heat and the careful preparation of the siegeworks, following in precision according to the hallowed ritual of the master, Sébastien de Vauban, who in the seventeenth century had made his name as the most celebrated of military engineers. The men worked on the batteries, the trenches, the connecting lines to more trenches and batteries, all working towards making a breach in the enemy's defences.

"On a May morning the siege began. There was a shattering roar. A shell had fallen on a rocket magazine inside Tippu's fort. Black smoke belched up in a huge plume, laced with fiery stars, plunging into shade the fort's long, low white walls, the shining roofs of Tippu's palace, the sugar-white minaret of his elegant mosque, the flat boulders of the river Cauvery which encircled the island of Seringapatam, and the shell-shattered trees, banks, and aloe hedges which concealed the British siege-works.

"By noon the next day, the breach was 'practicable,' and bamboo scaling-ladders were silently carried into the trenches at dusk.

"On the morning of fourth May, seventeen ninety-nine, the order went out for the assault."

"That came from General Sir David Baird," said Abigail, her eyes shining.

"You are remarkably well-informed," he commented.

"Go on," commanded Abigail.

He looked down at her doubtfully. "I am beginning to form an impression that you know as much as I do. But, very well.

"General Baird was in charge of the four thousand storming troops, and Wellesley was in charge of the reserve in the trenches. Baird shouted—"

" 'Now, my brave fellows, follow *me*, and prove yourselves worthy of the name of British soldiers!' " cried Abigail, doing a little dance of excitement.

He burst out laughing. "Now I *am* intrigued. How did you come by such a fund of masculine knowledge?"

"We have an unusual governess. We are too old, don't you know, to have a governess, and recently we have had few lessons, but our education has served to enliven the tedium of our country days."

"I find life in the country very busy."

"But you are a man! Men can ride and shoot and have jolly parties and go when and where they like. Ladies sit and sew and learn to prattle and flirt so that they may secure husbands."

Her shyness had gone. Her face, turned up to his, was animated. He realized with a little start that she was unaware of him as a man, only as a sort of companionable intelligence. And somehow that realization made him sharply aware of her as a desirable young woman. He had at first thought her a shy little thing, but now she was striding out beside him, quite unselfconsciously, and he realized her maidenly blushes had been because she had been caught out staring at her old home.

"Oh, we are nearly there," said Abigail. "You must leave me!"

"Will you save me a dance?" he called after her

flying figure but she did not appear to hear him. He mounted his horse and rode back to Hursley Park.

Lady Evans greeted him on his arrival with, "Well, did you see the famous Mannerling?"

"Fine in its way, but it did not appear anything extraordinary. On the other hand, I did have an extraordinary meeting."

"Not with the Deverses!"

"No, with one of the Beverley girls. Miss Abigail."

"Ah, yes, she has a twin. They are both nineteen. Was she making a call?"

"No, she was standing hanging on to the gates and gazing hungrily down the drive."

"Oh, dear."

"I spoke to her."

Lady Evans frowned her disapproval. "You had not been introduced."

"Miss Abigail was on her own, without maid or footman. I considered it my gentlemanly duty to walk her home."

"I hope you behaved yourself."

"Miss Abigail is the first young female I have ever come across who has not tried to flirt with me. On the other hand, she does seem to have a surprising knowledge of military history."

"Letitia," murmured Lady Evans with a reminiscent smile.

"I beg your pardon?"

"I am sorry, I was remembering someone like Miss Abigail I knew in the old days. I often thought she ruined her chances of marriage by being over-educated in masculine matters. She made every man who took an interest in her feel like a fool. The gentlemen do like to be petted and cajoled."

"I found Miss Abigail very refreshing."

"Not in danger of losing your heart?"

"Not I. The lady is nineteen and I am middle-aged."

"True, very true," said Lady Evans placidly. "I have the very lady in mind for you."

"Matchmaking? Who is this charmer?"

"Prudence Makepeace, twenty-five years of age and possessed of a great fortune, along with a great deal of common sense."

"And why is this great heiress unwed?"

"Her parents betrothed her to Charlie Tuffnel. He was killed in the Peninsular Wars."

"And she still mourns him?"

"That is the story her parents put about, but I find it hard to believe. She barely knew young Tuffnel. They were betrothed when they were children. One of those family arrangements. In any case, she arrives this very evening with her parents, so you may judge for yourself. They will stay with me until after the ball."

"Is she very ugly?"

Lady Evans laughed. "She is good and beautiful and wise."

"I cannot wait to meet this paragon. But with looks and money, if she has not yet been snapped up, there is something wrong."

"The same might be said of you," said Lady Evans tartly.

At that moment, while Lady Evans and Lord Burfield were talking, Harry Devers arrived home. He gazed about him lovingly as the peace of Mannerling enfolded him. He felt like a child being welcomed back into the loving embrace of a parent, for the house meant more to him now than his mother and father, who were seated in the drawing-room, nervously waiting to see if their son was as changed as he had claimed to be.

When he marched in and bowed formally to both of them, they studied his face for marks of dissipation, but Harry was looking fit and well.

Harry had gained in cunning. He never meant to be humiliated ever again the way he had been humiliated by Jessica Beverley's rejection of his suit. He also did not plan to annoy his father any further in case he found himself disinherited. He longed to resign from the army and planned to spend the whole of his leave working towards that end. If he took an interest in the estates, then surely they would let him stay.

He nearly forgot his good intentions when his mother said "I entertained the Beverley twins, Abigail and Rachel, to tea."

"The devil you did!" cried Harry wrathfully. "After what I have suffered at that family's hands. Forced to rejoin my regiment . . ."

His father's voice was like ice. "You were not only obliged to go back to the army because of your assault on Jessica Beverley but also because you sold property in London, signing my name, to entertain that whore of an opera singer you had in keeping."

With a supreme effort Harry remembered his aim to get out of the army for good. "I am so sorry, sir," he said contritely, adopting the "little boy" look which he knew usually went to his mother's heart. "It's the shame of it all, sir, that makes me long to blame someone, anyone else."

"Well, well," said his father, mollified, "we will say no more about the matter. Except for one thing. It would do you no harm to get on friendly terms with the Beverley family. If you do that, the locals will begin to think the scandal was blown out of all proportion and was all a hum."

"I will try," said Harry with every appearance of humility while he privately thought he would see the whole pack of Beverleys in hell first.

Lord Burfield descended to the drawing-room that evening to join his hostess and her new guests. He was, despite Lady Evans's description, prepared to find Miss Prudence Makepeace as someone quite plain and ordinary.

Prudence was standing by the fireplace, talking to Lady Evans. She had glossy brown hair, a creamy skin, large eyes, and a small mouth. Her figure was neat. She looked straight across at him and then delicately lowered her eyelids.

With that first sight of him, Prudence Makepeace had marked Lord Burfield down as her own. She had heard of his fortune, so he could not be damned as an adventurer, but she had not dreamed for one moment that he would turn out to be so devastatingly handsome. Prudence had had many opportunities to marry, but she had a high opinion of her own looks and intelligence and wanted only the best.

Lady Evans made the introductions. Mr. and Mrs. Makepeace were a comfortable-looking, undistinguished couple who were obviously rather in awe of their daughter. After some general conversation, Lord Burfield said to Prudence, "I was sorry to learn of your loss."

"Oh, you mean my fiancé? That was very sad," said Prudence. "I barely knew him. But it was sad all the same."

"Have you been in London recently?" asked Lord Burfield.

"We have just returned," said Prudence. She slowly waved an ostrich feather fan and her eyes flirted over the edge of it. "So tedious. I prefer the country."

"How refreshing," he said, not knowing that Prudence's mother had found out from Lady Evans that Lord Burfield preferred country life to city life. "I am so used to young ladies preferring a life of balls and parties."

"But there is so much to do in the country." She gave a tinkling laugh. "Papa says my interest in the estate is quite *masculine*."

Prudence had been well schooled in Lord Burfield's likes and dislikes. But anxious that he should not question her about estates management, about which she knew nothing at all, she moved quickly on to one of his other loves—fine porcelain.

"But my one reason for enjoying a visit to London is to find some thing to add to my porcelain collection."

"Indeed! It appears we have many tastes in common, Miss Makepeace. Did you acquire anything of interest on your last visit?"

"I bought two vases of Vincennes-Sèvres porcelain, two vases with a light-blue background. They are in the Etruscan style. I also bought a Vincennes-Sèvres barometer and thermometer, each with ornamentation and precious painting, a table made of Sèvres porcelain, a commode with porcelain inlay, and a painting by Van Loo on a porcelain plaque."

He raised his eyebrows and threw her a puzzled look. She could not have said anything wrong, thought Prudence. Had she not studied that boring history of porcelain from cover to cover?

"I do not know how such pieces came to be in England," said Lord Burfield. "These items are enumerated in Madame Du Barry's memoirs, and after her death, the rarest and most valuable, those you have just described, were declared national works of art by the French. May I ask in which sale-room you purchased them?"

"Not a sale-room," said Prudence quickly. "My father's agent bought them for me from a French émigré."

"Strange," he said, half to himself, and Prudence stifled a little sigh of relief when dinner was announced.

Unlike the Americans, who still kept to the old ways and had the sexes segregated at dinner, they all sat at the same table but with the ladies down one side and the gentlemen down the other.

Lady Evans kept a good table. The first course was green pea soup, removed with a haunch of lamb, larded and glazed with cucumber sauce, haricot of mutton, breast of veal and stewed peas, a sauté of sweetbreads and mushrooms, raised pie à la française, fricassee of chicken, neck of venison, beef olives and sauce piquant, and fish removed with rump of beef à la Mantua.

The second course consisted of larded guinea fowl, peas, blancmange, macaroni, currant-and-raspberry pie, omelette soufflé, chantilly cake, french beans, and hare.

Prudence, who actually had a notebook in her room in which she had written down all Lord Burfield's likes and dislikes, which her mother had gleaned from Lady Evans, had learned that he detested the modern fashion of ladies' picking at their food. So she ate with every appearance of a hearty appetite. But her trim figure owed more to tight lacing than nature and she began to feel her stays digging into her. Her face grew red and then white. A footman placed a portion of larded guinea fowl in front of her. She stared at it dismally and then fell into a dead faint, her head resting on her plate and the guinea fowl buried in her hair.

Footmen carried Prudence back into the drawing-room and laid her gently on the sofa. Lord Burfield had risen to his feet but Lady Evans snapped, "Do sit down, Rupert. Let the ladies cope with it." She knew just why Prudence had fainted, thought her a silly girl, but nonetheless considered her an excellent match for Lord Burfield and therefore did not want him to see any more of the girl when she had bits of guinea fowl in her hair and gravy running down her cheeks. The reason for Lady Evans's partiality was because, unknown to her, Prudence had a notebook on *her* likes and dislikes also in her room, her mother having told her that Lady Evans had influence with this Lord Burfield, and so Prudence had been able to charm Lady Evans shortly after her arrival by talking on topics dear to that lady's heart.

Lady Evans thought briefly of this Abigail Beverley who had made some sort of impression on Lord Burfield. But she was evidently highly well-informed and intelligent, and no gentleman liked that. Prudence, thought Lady Evans comfortably, was a sensible girl with a great deal of common sense, and common sense was a good thing but actual knowledge was a dangerous thing!

The day before the ball, Rachel was showing every sign that she would be well enough to go. She smiled at Abigail and said, "Miss Trumble has been an angel. She did manage to stop me fretting or I might have continued to be too ill." She looked curiously at her twin. "You have been very silent on the subject of the ball. Are you not excited?"

"We have been so long out of society," said Abigail, "that I fear I must have become accustomed to seeing no one."

"I asked for you a few days ago," said Rachel, still looking at her curiously, "and you could not be found. Miss Trumble feared you had disobeyed orders and gone out walking on your own. When you came to my room later you looked as if you had some secret you were not sharing with me. Where did you go?"

"I went to look at Mannerling," said Abigail reluctantly.

"Oh, you should not!" cried Rachel. "We have been such fools. I hope no one saw you."

"Someone did. A gentleman. A Lord Burfield. He is staying with Lady Evans."

"Dear me, Abigail, he will no doubt have heard the country gossip about us and will have already regaled Lady Evans and her other guests with a story about how he found you, unaccompanied, haunting your old home."

Abigail blushed.

"But perhaps," suggested Rachel hopefully, "you did not tell him who you were."

"I am afraid I did, and yes, he evidently knew all about us and he said Mannerling did not look anything out of the common way to him."

"Oh, dear." Rachel had conjured up a picture in her mind of this Lord Burfield as an elderly gentleman. "Why on earth did you go to Mannerling, Abigail? We must put all that behind us. We are comfortable here, and Mama must have money to buy those splendid ball gowns. We shall be all the crack again."

But Abigail was not comforted by that thought.

She was beginning to dread this ball. She had enjoyed Lord Burfield's company but now the thought of him talking about seeing her at Mannerling was making her begin to fear the looks and contemptuous stares she was now sure would be cast in her direction.

When the Beverley sisters were gathered in the parlour ready to set out for the ball, Miss Trumble beamed on them with pride. Even Lizzie, who was never accounted much of a beauty because of her red hair, looked ethereal in leaf-green muslin with a wreath of ivy leaves in her hair. Belinda was in blue muslin, her black hair shining under a little Juliet cap. Rachel and Abigail were both wearing white muslin, but Abigail's was trimmed at the neck and hem with little silk rosebuds and she wore a coronet of silk rosebuds on her head, and Rachel's gown was trimmed with silk ears of corn. She wore a gold circlet on her hair, which Miss Trumble had dressed in one of the latest Roman styles. Miss Trumble had been determined that, on this great occasion, the twins should not be dressed alike.

But Lady Beverley could only see that her daughters were not bedecked in precious jewels as they had been at the great balls at Mannerling, and Miss Trumble's quiet remark that no young unmarried miss was expected to wear any ornaments grander than coral or seed-pearls did not seem to comfort her.

They were helped into their warm cloaks, shawls, and wraps by the maids.

It was a frosty, moonlit night, and the horses pulling the rented coach struck sparks from the hard road with their hooves.

Lady Beverley was in a bad mood. Her parsimony

had made her stop short at ordering a new ensemble for herself, for she considered her plum velvet gown and velvet turban, which had served her for several years, fine enough. But her nose was put out of joint by her governess's modish gown of lilac satin and lilac silk turban with a dyed ostrich feather curled round the edge. Lady Beverley did not like the idea of being outshone by a servant. She contented herself by saying she was sure dear Lady Evans must have made a mistake and would be shocked to see a mere governess arriving as a guest.

When they alighted from the carriage, the girls stood for a moment looking up at the house. It was a large Elizabethan mansion with many mullioned windows. "Quite fine in its way" said Belinda, "but not a patch on Mannerling."

"No," agreed Miss Trumble, "I doubt if this pleasant mansion has the power to turn intelligent young ladies into silly misses!"

"Remember your place, Miss Trumble," said Lady Beverley awfully. "You are not allowed to make sneering remarks about the great house that was once ours."

Miss Trumble ignored her and followed her charges into a vast gloomy entrance hall, smelling of woodsmoke and damp dog. They left their cloaks and wraps in a room off the hall and then were led through a chain of corridors to the ballroom, which was a modern extension added to the back of the old house. Miss Trumble hoped she had schooled her girls in etiquette as diligently as she had schooled them in learning. There were many offences against English manners which could be committed by the unwary foreigner or the green girl. The three greatest were these: never put your knife in your mouth instead of your fork; never take up sugar or asparagus with your fingers: and *never* spit anywhere in the room. An adventurer in London society actually went undetected and was able to pass himself off as a man of rank because of the single circumstance of picking up an olive with his fork rather than his fingers. Tremendous importance was attached to trivia.

The ballroom was large and square, with a chalked floor and two fireplaces at either end. Branches of candles burnt on the walls and a great candelabrum blazed overhead. Despite the chill of the evening outside, the room was very warm indeed.

Lord Burfield, looking across the room, was in no doubt that the Beverley sisters had arrived, even though he did not recognize Abigail at first glance. Their beauty outshone that of every other lady in the room. It was not so much their looks as a sort of radiance that surrounded them. He had thought Abigail a very pretty girl when he had met her outside Mannerling. Now, as he singled her out from the others, he thought her quite the most beautiful creature he had ever seen.

Prudence, too, had noticed the arrival of these charmers. "Find out who they are?" she whispered to her mother.

"I have just heard someone remark that they are the famous Beverley sisters."

"Famous for what?"

"Beauty," said her mother tactlessly.

Prudence's eyes went to Lord Burfield's handsome face. He, too, was watching the Beverley sisters, but the one which seemed to intrigue him most was the fair one with the rosebuds in her hair. Prudence became determined to find out as much as she could about these sisters. Know your enemy, she thought.

Her hand was claimed for a dance by Lord Burfield. It was the quadrille. Prudence, like many young ladies, had been trained in the intricate steps of the quadrille by a dancing master, and although she performed them exactly, she was rather heavy on her feet and apt to come down from one of the leaps in the air with a thump. She had no opportunity to talk to Lord Burfield until they were promenading round the floor at the end of the dance. The promenade, where one strolled in a circle with one's partner before the next dance, was a great opportunity for flirtation.

"You are looking very fine tonight, Miss Makepeace," said Lord Burfield gallantly. Prudence was wearing white muslin with many frills and it was bound at the waist with a frilly edged sash. She had a tall head-dress of osprey feathers.

"I am surprised you even noticed my appearance, my lord. Your attention appeared to be caught by the Beverley sisters."

He smiled down at her but did not reply.

"Do they live locally?"

"I believe so," he said.

"Do they do the Season?"

"Miss Makepeace, I confess to being remarkably ill-informed on the subject of the Beverleys. I suggest you ask one of them all about themselves."

Mrs. Makepeace, on the other hand, was being very well informed on that very subject by Hedgefield's prize gossip, Miss Turlow, who had been snubbed by the Beverleys in the days of their wealth. Mrs. Makepeace listened with rapt and flattering attention to the tale of this once-proud family. When Miss Turlow had finished, Mrs. Makepeace put up her quizzing-glass and studied the sisters. "If they are as poor as you say," she said, "why is it that their gowns have obviously been made for them by one of the finest dressmakers?"

Miss Turlow knew that she had never seen the girls wear those gowns before but her spite would not allow her to say so. "I believe they still have a vast wardrobe from a few years ago," she remarked.

Lady Evans, in the meantime, had realized that whatever game Letitia Trumble was playing she would need to go along with it and not acknowledge her as a friend, but she wondered where she had gone. Miss Trumble had arrived with the Beverley party. But then she had disappeared from view.

Lady Evans approached Lady Beverley and asked, "Where is Miss Trumble?"

"My governess?" Lady Beverley gave a condescending little laugh. "I felt she was a trifle *de trop* and so I sent her to wait in the hall."

Lady Beverley had thought she had suffered enough when two guests had approached and had addressed Miss Trumble as Lady Beverley, and so she had sent her away.

"Miss Trumble was invited as a guest, Lady Beverley," said old Lady Evans haughtily. "In fact, it was because of Miss Trumble's request that your daughters were invited here at all. Be so good as to remember that!"

Lady Evans swept off. I must get rid of Miss Trumble, thought Lady Beverley angrily. She is nothing more than a servant. How very odd of Lady Evans! But then she is so very old. Her wits must be wandering.

Lady Evans went through to the hall. Miss Trumble was sitting on a hard chair, reading a book.

"Letitia," hissed Lady Evans, "come back to the

ballroom immediately. I was forced to remind your employer that it was thanks to you that the Beverleys are here at all."

Miss Trumble put away her book in her reticule and stood up and shook down the folds of her gown. "How very loyal you are. But I fear Lady Beverley will send me packing."

"And so . . . and so what is that to you?"

"Humour me. I am fond of my girls."

"Very well. But it annoys me to see you treated thus."

As they walked together towards the ballroom, Miss Trumble said, "That is a fine-looking man, the one with the fair hair, the tall one in the black coat and silk knee-breeches with the sapphire stickpin in his cravat."

"That must be Lord Burfield. He is staying with me. Ah, no, Letitia, I have chosen a very proper young heiress for him."

"Is he short of funds?"

"On the contrary, and therefore it is safe and suitable that he should marry money."

"Dear me, what a mercenary world we live in. Ah, here we are and there is my employer looking daggers at me."

Old Lady Evans looked amused. "If you will insist on wearing a finer gown than your employer, Letitia, it is no wonder the lady dislikes you. I see all your young ladies have partners, but you will find it hard to get husbands for them."

"I am not so sure about that," said Miss Trumble. "The two elder girls did well for themselves."

Lady Evans noticed that Lord Burfield was dancing again with Prudence and frowned. That made two dances. He could not, therefore, dance with her again, and it was not yet the supper dance.

Lord Burfield had remarked the startling likeness of the Beverley twins, and yet felt he would be able to tell Abigail from Rachel quite easily. Abigail had the more dominating personality. Rachel was quieter, more subdued, quite shy.

He found Prudence a pleasant sort of lady, just the sort he ought to marry. She would run his home well, and she was past the first blush of youth and would therefore be more sensible than any flighty young girl.

He had not really meant to ask Abigail for the supper dance but somehow he found himself doing just that. He performed a country dance with her, noticing how light and graceful she was. When he led her to the supper-room, she seemed very much at ease with him, and that caused him a slight feeling of pique. He wondered what it would take to make Miss Abigail Beverley aware of him as a man.

When they had been served with food and wine, Abigail asked, "Did you leave the army before the start of the Peninsular Wars?"

"No, I served there as well."

"Is there a great deal of hardship for such as you, marching so long and fighting so hard?"

"It varies, Miss Abigail. Sometimes it was hard to find a dry place to pass the night. I remember when a Colonel Freemantle was sent ahead during the retreat of the army from Burgos to find accommodation for Wellington himself. All he could find was a simple hut. He had a fire lit and then scrawled a message on the door that the hut was reserved for Wellington, but when he returned later to the hut, he found an officer warming himself by the fire and refusing to move, 'not even for Wellington, not even for Old Nick himself.' The officer, however, moved when he was threatened with arrest. The story was repeated at White's, where our celebrated Beau Brummel exclaimed to Freemantle, 'If I had been in your place, Freemantle, I should have rung the bell and had the fellow kicked downstairs by the servants,' which shows how little some of our dandies know about campaigning. But tell me something of yourself, Miss Abigail. Do you go to London?"

"I shall never see London again," said Abigail gloomily. "We used to go when Isabella was making her come-out and I loved the theatres and plays, the parks and the people. It must be fine to be able to visit London, particularly in the winter. The nights are so long and dark, and we have to be abed so early."

"And why is that?"

"To save candles." Abigail bit her lip and blushed, cursing her mother's parsimony in her heart. What would he think of a family who saved candles like the veriest peasant?

"I saw a very good performance of Falstaff when I was last in London," he said quickly. "Kean was playing him and was quite brilliant. He caught the finest shades of the character."

"I feel some actors forget that Falstaff, although a man of vulgar soul, is still by habit and inclination a practised courtier," said Abigail eagerly, "and the coarseness he often assumes in the prince's company is at least as much intentional acting, employed by him to amuse the prince, as to gratify his own humour."

"You have the right of it," said Lord Burfield, signalling to a footman to pour more wine for them. "The way Kean portrayed him, at first you see a facetious man, ludicrously fat, but a man of dignified and gentlemanlike air, always a joker, it is true, but good *ton*. In the second stage, he allows himself to take all sorts of freedoms but with every care to exalt the prince and to assume only the privilege of a court fool who *apparently* may say all that comes into his head. In the last stage, we see Falstaff in complete 'negligé,' after he has thrown off all regard to good appearances, and yet he still remains original and excites more laughter than disgust. Shakespeare's genius never fails to amaze me. As Sir Walter Scott so prettily puts it, 'I can only compare Shakespeare with that man in the *Arabian Nights* who has the power of passing into any body with ease, and imitating its feelings and actions.'

"But back to the play. It concluded with a melodrama in which a large Newfoundland dog really acted admirably. He defended a banner for a long time, pursued by the enemy, and afterwards came on the stage wounded, lame and bleeding, and died in the most masterly manner, with a last wag of his tail, which was really full of genius."

"The dog did not *really* die?" asked Abigail anxiously.

"No, that animal was as fine an actor as Kean. Besides, the audience would not have minded a human being, or a bear or a bull actually dying on the stage, but not a dog like that."

"How exciting and wonderful it all sounds," said Abigail wistfully. "Miss Trumble reads us the plays of Shakespeare and we often act the parts, but it is not the same as seeing one. Do you have a busy social life in London?"

"I do what everyone does," said Lord Burfield,

meaning every man in society. "I rise late, read three or four newspapers at breakfast. I look in my visiting-book to see what calls I have to pay, and either drive to pay them in my curricle, or ride. At this time of year, I am sometimes startled by beauty even in dingy London. The struggle of the blood-red sun with the winter fogs can often produce wild and singular effects of light. I return when it is dark, work a little at my papers, dress for dinner, which is now at seven or eight, and then usually spend the evening at the theatre or at some small party or rout, but usually I avoid routs. One hardly finds standing room and is pushed and pulled in a hothouse atmosphere. But small parties are not very enlivening either. There is no general conversation. Each gentleman singles out the lady of his choice and talks to her all evening. Everyone talks French 'tant bien que mal,' but this annoys the ladies after a time and any gentleman who sticks to English can be sure of a good reception."

"And do you often find a lady who pleases you enough to sit with her all evening?" asked Abigail, her motive for asking the question owing all to curiosity and none to flirtation.

He smiled into her eyes, "Not until this very night, Miss Abigail."

The compliment was insincere, but then so were most of the compliments bandied about society. Seeing the little flicker of disappointment in him in her large blue eyes, he was about to try to reclaim her good opinion when he realized the lady on his other side was trying to catch his attention. He turned reluctantly towards her. Abigail turned her attention to the gentleman on her other side and appeared, thought Lord Burfield a little sourly, to be keeping him well amused.

From across the room, Prudence flirted and charmed *her* companion while, from under her lashes, she covertly watched Lord Burfield and felt a sense of relief when he finally turned away to speak to the lady on his other side. She had not liked the way that he and Abigail Beverley had been talking. She could not hear a word they had been saying, but she sensed a rapport between them.

Lord Burfield had danced two whole dances with her and therefore could not ask for another. Then she remembered that she and her parents were supposed to stay with Lady Evans only until after the ball. Lord Burfield was staying longer. She must get her parents to suggest they stay longer themselves. She bit her lip. Lord Burfield had danced with Abigail and had taken her in to supper. Therefore he would call on her the following day to pay his respects. In town, gentlemen often sent a servant with a card instead. But this was the country.

There must be some way she could stop him from going. But what? If she locked him in his room, all he had to do was to ring the bell or shout for the servants. Her mother had a bottle of laudanum. She could drug him so that he would sleep through the day. Perhaps that was the answer. But what opportunity would she have? Perhaps when the ball was finally over and the guests had departed, she could suggest the tea-tray be brought in. Too difficult. "Oh, sir, you do flatter me so," she said to the gentleman next to her, only dimly having heard a compliment.

Perhaps, her mind raced, she could ask him later

in the evening to fetch her a glass of lemonade.
There was another room off the ballroom where
maids served light snacks, sandwiches, and refresh-
ments of all description right throughout the ball.
She had noticed that gentlemen usually brought
themselves a glass of champagne or wine at the same
time as they fetched a drink for the lady. If she could
then introduce laudanum into his glass, he would be
forced to retire and sleep too long the next day to go
on calls.

As soon as the supper was over, she slipped
upstairs to her mother's room and seized the bottle
of laudanum and slipped it down the front of her
dress.

She danced with partner after partner, all the
while covertly watching her quarry. When she was
promenading after a cotillion which she had been
dancing but Lord Burfield had not, she saw him
standing outside the refreshment room. She murmured to her partner that she must go and repair a
rent in her gown. Instead she made her way to Lord
Burfield's side and said, "I am so very thirsty.
Would you be so kind as to fetch me a glass of
lemonade?"

"Your servant," he said, bowed and went off to the
refreshment room. Prudence took a quick look
around and fished the bottle out of her corsage. But
one person was watching her curiously. Lizzie, tired
of dancing, was sitting quietly on a little chair
behind a marble statue in a corner of the room. This
was more interesting than dancing, thought Lizzie.
Why should that lady look so furtive? Why had she
taken that little green bottle out of the neck of her
gown and concealed it in her hand?

Lizzie saw Lord Burfield come back with a little

tray which held two glasses of lemonade. She saw him say something to Prudence, although she did not yet know their names, and then the couple walked together to where there were two seats in front of the statue behind which Lizzie was seated. Lizzie edged her chair to the side until she could see the couple. The man set the little tray on a small table beside them. The lady suddenly gave a shriek of laughter and said "Do but look at that quiz over there, Lord Burfield!"

"Where, Miss Makepeace?"

"Why, over there by the fireplace near the entrance!"

Lord Burfield raised his quizzing-glass. Prudence quickly emptied most of the contents of the little bottle into his glass.

Lizzie stared wide-eyed. Was this Miss Makepeace trying to poison this Lord Burfield? Or was it a love potion?

She did not want to make a scene. But she left her seat, leaned round the statue, and in a moment had turned the little tray around.

"Your lemonade, Miss Makepeace," said Lord Burfield.

Prudence drank hers with a long gulp, anxious to show that she had really been thirsty. He sipped his, looking as if he did not like it very much.

But then Prudence began to feel groggy. At first she was bewildered, wondering whether her stays had been lashed too tight, but with the last of her wits she realized she had drunk the glass with the laudanum in it. She got to her feet. Lord Burfield rose as well. "Excuse me," muttered Prudence. He watched her anxiously as she swayed off, colliding with some of the guests.

"Now what have I done?" said a conscience-stricken little voice at his elbow.

He looked down into the face of the youngest of the Beverley sisters. "What have you done?"

"That lady with you," said Lizzie earnestly, "took a bottle out of her corsage and poured the contents into your glass, so I turned the tray around. I thought it was a love potion. But what if it was poison?"

He remembered with alarm Prudence's odd exit from the ballroom. "I had better find out," he said.

He could hardly believe this odd little girl's strange story, but he approached Mrs. Makepeace and said she should find her daughter, for he feared she was unwell. "Perhaps she has gone to her room," said Mrs. Makepeace anxiously. She hurried off and Lord Burfield followed her as she made her way through the twisting passages of the old house and then up the staircase to the bedrooms. Mrs. Makepeace went into her daughter's bedroom. Prudence was lying face down on the bed. She turned her over. A small snore sounded. Mrs. Makepeace could not believe that Prudence had actually fallen asleep. She was about to ring for the maid to come and undress her daughter when she noticed a little bottle lying next to Prudence's open hand. She picked it up and recognized the laudanum bottle. What had the child been about to take laudanum? Nothing could be done until the girl woke up and could be questioned.

She rang for the maid and said tetchily in a voice that carried to Lord Burfield's listening ears, "Miss Prudence for some reason has taken a draught of laudanum. Be so good as to undress her." She went out of the bedroom and nearly collided with Lord Burfield.

"Oh, my lord," she said, colouring guiltily. "I am afraid my Prudence must have been overcome by the excitement of the ball. She is such a sensitive and delicate child. She is fast asleep! Pray return with me belowstairs."

Lord Burfield followed her back to the ballroom, his mind racing. Why had Prudence tried to drug him? He saw the small red-haired Beverley girl watching him anxiously and went to join her. "Laudanum," he murmured, "but let it be our secret. Which Beverley are you?"

"Lizzie."

"Then, Miss Lizzie, I am very much in your debt. I am Burfield."

"I know who you are," said Lizzie. "I asked Miss Trumble, my governess."

"You did not tell her the reason for your curiosity?"

"No, I was so afraid, you see, that it might have been poison."

"Well, let us say no more about it."

"Some ladies are, I believe," said Lizzie, her green eyes glittering like emeralds, "monstrous addicted to laudanum."

"That may be the case."

"But then, why would she put it in your glass?"

"I shall find out on the morrow, believe me."

"And if I keep your secret, will you tell me? You will be calling on Abigail, no doubt."

"I promise."

"Perhaps that is the reason she may have tried to drug you."

"What reason, pray?"

"To stop you calling on Abigail."

"I am sure that cannot be the case. Who would go to such lengths?"

Perhaps Prudence Makepeace, thought Lizzie, but she did not say so aloud.

# Chapter Three

*The ennui, which seizes me in such an indifferent state of mind, is too clearly written on my undiplomatic face not to extend to others as contagiously as yawning.*
—PRINCE PÜCKLER-MUSKAU

ABIGAIL BEGAN TO wonder when her mother intended to leave. The ballroom was beginning to become thin of company but Lady Beverley sat on, talking to a group of chaperones and dowagers with more animation than she had shown in some time. The clock on one of the walls showed it was four in the morning. The footmen were beginning to look jaded. Little Lizzie was sitting on her own in a corner, her eyes drooping. Abigail's feet in their white kid dancing slippers were aching.

She finished promenading with her partner and was crossing the floor to join Lizzie when Lord Burfield came up to her. "The honour of another dance, Miss Abigail?"

"If I must."

He raised his eyebrows. "You are ungracious."

"I am so very tired, my lord, and Mama shows no sign of leaving."

"Dance with me and then I will persuade Lady Evans to send you and your family on your way."

She smiled up at him. He put his hand at her waist and led her into the steps of the waltz. Abigail did not experience any of the delicious sensations a young lady should feel when waltzing with the most handsome man in the room. All she knew was that she felt comfortable with him, as if she had known him for a long time. She was so weary she was unaware of the speculative looks being cast in their direction. *Three* dances with the same young lady was considered tantamount to a proposal of marriage.

One of the fires had begun to smoke and the candle-light and colours of the jewels and gowns glimmered through the resultant dreamlike haze. When the waltz was over, she placed one gloved hand on Lord Burfield's arm and walked round the room with him. "Please, please try to get us to leave," she whispered. "I do not want to dance again."

"And after waltzing with you, every other dance would be an anticlimax," he said.

She looked up at him, slightly puzzled, and then her face cleared. "Oh, you are *flirting*. I am so sorry. I am too tired to flirt."

So much for my famous charm, thought Lord Burfield wryly. He pressed her hand. "Go and join your little sister, who is hiding in the corner, and I will talk to Lady Evans."

Abigail went up to Lizzie and sat down on a chair beside her. "Are we never going to leave?" said Lizzie, stifling a yawn.

"It will be all right soon," said Abigail. "Lord Burfield has gone to talk to Lady Evans and she will persuade Mama to take us away."

"Lord Burfield is charming and handsome, is he not?"

"I suppose he is."

"We are supposed to be looking for husbands,"

said Lizzie. "Had you not thought of him in that light?"

"No," said Abigail truthfully. "It is because of Mannerling."

"Oh, no. Not Mannerling still!"

"I mean, we have been such fools over that place, always hoping to marry to reclaim it, and now that I no longer think about the place, I cannot really, this early, begin to think of anything else. Also, I appear to lack romanticism in my character. When I think of marriage now, I feel a great weariness, a sort of oh-I-suppose-I-must. Believe me, were we still in funds, I might contemplate a future of spinsterhood with equanimity. You are still too young, Lizzie, to feel the pressures of needing to wed."

"I dream of having a place of my very own," said Lizzie. "The husband is always a shadowy figure. But I do dream of a trim house, with a pony and some dogs and perhaps children."

"There is Mama looking for us, and Miss Trumble," said Abigail. "She is saying something to Miss Trumble and Miss Trumble has that closed look on her face she always has when she is upset."

The reason for Miss Trumble's upset became all too apparent when they were all in the carriage and on the journey home. "Miss Trumble will be leaving us tomorrow," said Lady Beverley. "You girls no longer need a governess."

"But who will look after us when we are ill?" wailed Lizzie. "Oh, Miss Trumble, you promised to stay with me till I wed!"

"I am sorry," said Miss Trumble quietly. "I have no choice in the matter."

"But where will you go?" asked Belinda.

"I shall go as companion to Lady Evans."

Lady Beverley's pale gaze fastened on the governess's face. "And when was this arranged, pray?"

"What I do or do not do is no longer any business of yours," said Miss Trumble with hauteur.

Abigail said, "I do not know what we will do without you, who we will lean on. It is too bad of you, Mama. I know what it is! Miss Trumble was wearing a finer gown than yours and you took a pet and it is all your own fault, for you could have ordered a new dress for yourself."

"Silence!" commanded Lady Beverley. "Miss Trumble is leaving tomorrow, and that is that!"

The next day the sisters arose late. When they gathered downstairs it was to find that the gentlemen they had danced with the night before had sent cards, which meant they would not be calling in person, and only Lizzie noticed that Lord Burfield alone had not sent his card.

Miss Trumble's trunks were packed, corded, and standing in the hall. The day was grey and cold, with a chill wind from the north-east. Lady Beverley was staying in her room, so it was left to the sisters to say goodbye to their governess. How they had often resented her lessons and homilies, and yet how bereft they felt as her slim figure climbed into the carriage beside a gloomy Barry Wort.

"We cannot really manage without you," said Abigail. "Will you come back and see us?"

"I doubt if your mama would allow that," said Miss Trumble, smiling down at their sorrowful faces. "But I will write to you."

"You are only going as far as Lady Evans's home. We could call on you," said Lizzie eagerly.

"I am afraid that would not be suitable," replied Miss Trumble. "Goodbye, my chucks, be good."

Clustered outside the door, they watched sadly as Barry clicked his tongue and the little open carriage moved off down the short drive.

There was a short silence and then Barry said, "I reckon I'll write to Miss Isabella, I mean Lady Fitzpatrick, and tell her I will join her lord's household in Ireland."

"Oh, no, you must not do that, Barry."

"But you will be gone."

Miss Trumble gave a little smile. "Only for a little, Barry. Only for a little."

Lord Burfield drove past Barry and Miss Trumble on his way to Brookfield House. He recognized the governess and touched his hat. He saw the trunks piled up in the rumble. Lady Evans had told him before he left that she had engaged the Beverleys' governess as companion.

He was surprised when he reached Brookfield House to find it a trim mansion with well-kept gardens. Barry had done much to bring the house and grounds into good repair. From the stories about the Beverleys, he had expected to find them living in shabby circumstances.

The fact that he was not expected, that no callers had been expected, was evident, firstly, in the flustered mien of the little maid who answered the door to him. He was led into a chilly, little-used drawing-room while another maid struggled to make up the fire. The maid then went upstairs and scratched on the door of Lady Beverley's bedroom and then entered.

"Beg pardon, my lady," she whispered to the figure on the bed, "but Lord Burfield is called."

"I cannot see him," wailed Lady Beverley. "I have the headache. Send Miss Trumble to me."

"Miss Trumble has left."

Lady Beverley groaned. "Miss Trumble often made me a posset. Ask Josiah to make me one the same and bring it to me and present my apologies to Lord Burfield."

The maid, Betty, anxious to please her mistress above all else, went first to the kitchen, where Josiah told her that Miss Trumble had made all possets, tisanes, and medicines herself and he did not have the recipes. That intelligence was immediately conveyed to her ladyship, who groaned again.

Lord Burfield sat on in the chilly drawing-room and wondered if anyone intended to acknowledge his presence. At last he knelt down in front of the fire, which had gone out and set about relighting it until there was a comfortable blaze. He was rubbing his hands fastidiously with a cambric handkerchief edged with lace when the door opened and Abigail came in.

"I heard the crackling of the fire and wondered who was here," she said cheerfully. "How good of you to call. We did not expect you, don't you know, because we are not considered marriageable because of our reduced circumstances, and so gentlemen send cards instead. I shall call the others. No, on second thoughts, why do you not join us in the parlour? We do not entertain much—well, not at all, to be honest with you—and the parlour is much more comfortable. This drawing-room has not been fired this age and is damp."

He followed her out and into a cheerful little par-

62

lour. The other three sisters were grouped around the fire. They rose at his entrance and curtsied prettily.

The room was cheerful and filled with books and sewing. Bowls of pot-pourri scented the air. The chairs were worn but comfortable and he took a large armchair by the fire. Cushions were placed at his back and the maids were sent scurrying to fetch cakes and tea.

"It is too cold to leave the door standing ajar," said Abigail. "But then you are not alone with one of us, Lord Burfield, and so we shall all chaperon each other."

Abigail was wearing an old blue woollen gown, a trifle short on her, but showing she had excellent ankles. The blue of the gown highlighted the intense blue of her eyes and the creaminess of her skin. She perched unselfconsciously on the arm of his chair and smiled down at him with open friendliness.

"You are to be our Scheherazade on this dreary afternoon," said Abigail. "We expect lots of stories."

Lizzie sat on a footstool at his feet, Belinda and Rachel sat on a sofa opposite him, not a fashionable backless sofa but a comfortably well-stuffed one, covered in rose-patterned chintz.

"I only meant to call for the regulation ten minutes," said Lord Burfield, stretching out his booted feet to the cheerful blaze of the fire. "But perhaps, when I have had tea, I will tell you some stories."

So tea was brought in and placed on a low table in front of the fire. Abigail rose to make the tea, taking the place of mistress of the house. Tea-making was too delicate a ritual to be left to the maids.

Once Lord Burfield had been served with tea and cakes, they all looked at him with the bright inquisitiveness of birds. He gave a reluctant laugh. "What sort of stories would you like to hear?"

"About your battles," said Lizzie, who had heard at the ball that he had been a soldier.

He was about to protest that such stories were not for delicate ears but then he recalled how well-informed Abigail had appeared to be and so he began, half-humorously at first and then more seriously as he lost himself in the past. The afternoon wore on. More candles and lamps were lit and he realized with a little start of surprise that he had never talked so much about himself in his life before, and to a roomful of young misses, too.

He felt at home and at ease and when Lizzie, at the end of his tales, suggested a game of Pope Joan, he found himself agreeing and then moved into the dining-room with them to share a modest but well-cooked dinner. Every time he thought of returning to Lady Evans and Prudence Makepeace, he experienced a feeling of boredom. He had not enjoyed himself so much in such a long time, nor had he felt so much at home. Prudence had not been awake when he had left, so he had whispered to Lizzie he did not know the reason for her odd action.

Miss Trumble had been an interested audience to Prudence's explanation that she had been suffering from the headache and had taken that bottle of laudanum from her mother's room to help the pain. Mrs. Makepeace's pained inquiries as to why she had chosen to take the stuff and pour it into a glass of lemonade which Lord Burfield had brought her and Prudence's subsequent and petulant inquiries as to what could possibly be keeping Lord Burfield at the Beverleys led the shrewd Miss Trumble to believe that Prudence had meant to drug Lord Burfield to prevent him calling on the Beverleys and had drunk the stuff herself by accident. Prudence, on being initially introduced to Miss Trumble, had haughtily given that lady two fingers to shake and then had cut her dead. Then she became aware that Lady Evans appeared inordinately fond of this new companion of hers and so, after her "confession" was over, she began to study Miss Trumble. Miss Trumble had been the Beverleys' governess and therefore would be a good source of information about them.

She therefore decided to befriend this old creature, thinking that the condescension of a few friendly words would be enough, but found all her initial approaches being met with the stately haughtiness of a duchess.

A note was brought in just before dinner and handed to Lady Evans, who read it and said, "We must not wait dinner for Lord Burfield. He is dining out this evening."

Miss Trumble rose quickly to her feet and hurried out. Prudence murmured an excuse herself and rapidly followed her. Her light slippers making no sound on the stairs, Prudence scurried after Miss Trumble. She saw that lady move quickly out of the front door and heard her call sharply, "Barry!"

Prudence went as far as the open doorway and looked out. By the light of an oil-lamp over the door she could see Miss Trumble talking to a servant, and not a liveried servant either.

"Barry," Miss Trumble was saying, although the frustrated Prudence could not hear the words, "how are things?"

"Gloomy after you left, miss," said Barry, "and my lady in bed with the headache and none of your cures to soothe her. Lord Burfield is being vastly entertained by the young ladies and is staying for dinner."

"He took Abigail into supper last night," said Miss Trumble. "That looks hopeful. He is an eminently suitable man."

Barry grinned. "Anyone other than Harry Devers."

"Anyone other than him," agreed Miss Trumble.

"Don't turn round now, miss," said Barry, "but there is a young lady hiding in the shadows of the doorway watching us but she is too far away to hear what we are saying."

"That will be a Miss Prudence Makepeace," said Miss Trumble equably. "She followed me down. She is anxious to secure Lord Burfield for herself."

"Do you think she will?"

"Perhaps. She appears most determined. In fact, I believe she attempted to drug Lord Burfield with laudanum at the ball last night so that he would be unable to call on the Beverleys today."

"Do be careful, miss, she might put something in your drink."

"I shall be careful. Do let me know if anything untoward occurs at Brookfield House, Barry."

Miss Trumble drew back. Barry touched his hat and drove off. Miss Trumble turned back to the house, feeling somewhat dejected. She missed the girls.

When she walked back into the house, there was no sign of Prudence, that young lady having run ahead of her and up the stairs.

Prudence was all too anxious to convey the intelligence to Lady Evans that her new companion had sneaked downstairs to talk to a low servant.

She found an opportunity after dinner. Lady Evans listened to her carefully and then said, "The note was brought from Brookfield House, where Miss Trumble was so recently employed. It is natural in

66

her to want to know how the family is faring without her. What is not natural, Miss Makepeace, is that you should spy on her."

Prudence turned scarlet. "I was not spying on her!" she exclaimed. "I felt over-warm and merely stepped outside before dinner for a breath of fresh air and happened to come across her."

"Indeed," said Lady Evans cynically. "Heed a word of advice from an old lady, child. You will not secure the attentions of Lord Burfield by plotting and scheming. Try to be more natural."

"I was not . . ." began Prudence, but Lady Evans walked away as she was protesting and joined Miss Trumble on the sofa.

"I cannot like that young lady," murmured Miss Trumble.

"Prudence will do very well for Burfield," said Lady Evans. "I know you would like to see the Beverley girls settled, but Burfield's parents would not thank me for finding him a penniless parti."

"I am not at all sure that the Beverleys are penniless," said Miss Trumble. "Because of their recent ruin, Lady Beverley has become a trifle parsimonious."

"Then who would want such as she as a mother-in-law?" demanded Lady Evans.

Miss Trumble bit back a sigh. It would be better to forget about the Beverleys for a little. If it was meant by the fates that Abigail should marry Lord Burfield, then that would happen. And if Lord Burfield chose to ally himself with such as Prudence Makepeace, then he was not good enough for Abigail.

It was unfortunate for Abigail that her mother recovered enough to join them after dinner. She immediately declared herself amazed that Lord Burfield should have stayed for dinner when her daughters were not chaperoned. She complained loudly of her headache, she complained that she had not been informed that Lord Burfield had decided to stay longer than any gentleman making a call should.

And so Lord Burfield bowed his way out, as glad to make his escape as he had been earlier glad to stay. On the road home, he remembered all the tales he had heard of the Beverleys and once again saw in his mind's eye Abigail standing outside the gates of Mannerling. He knew friends who had made disastrous marriages into bad families because they had been seduced by beauty, rather than character. He was suddenly anxious to return to his own home, his own lands, and forget any ideas of marriage for the time being.

On the following day, Prudence struck him as being so amiable and compliant and her parents so staid and respectable that he found himself issuing an invitation to them to visit him the following month at his home. Lady Evans was pleased. The invitation was virtually to a proposal of marriage.

"He is not in love with her and never will be," said Miss Trumble sadly.

Lady Evans snorted with contempt. "What has love got to do with marriage, Letitia? Look what misery love brought you!"

And Miss Trumble bowed her head and did not reply.

Harry Devers was bored. He knew he was being socially shunned by the county and he did not like it one bit. He had suggested giving a party, for he was becoming increasingly obsessed with the grandeur of Mannerling and wished to show the house off, but his father had pointed out that few would attend. He was still in bad odour. In order to get rid of his feelings of frustration and anger, he went out riding one frosty afternoon, driving his horse hard over hedges and ditches until, near Brookfield House, the tired animal could take no more and stopped dead at a fence. Harry shot over its head, struck his head on a stone and lay still.

Abigail and Rachel were out walking in the frosty countryside. There was a chill wind carrying a metallic smell which threatened snow to come. Behind them walked the maid Betty, who was feeling tired and grumpy. She did not share the girl's enthusiasm for long walks. At times, she was elevated to the grand position of lady's-maid, but mostly she was treated by Lady Beverley as a maid of all work. Betty missed Miss Trumble's encouragement and calm good sense. The household was not the same. To her relief, she heard Abigail say to Rachel, "I think we should turn back now."

Rachel looked up at the lowering sky and agreed, "It is getting dark and I think it may snow before nightfall."

"Listen!" said Abigail, stopping short. "What is that sound? Like moaning."

"The wind," suggested Rachel.

"No, there it is again. From over there. Probably some poor animal caught in a trap."

Betty shivered. "That'll be one of farmer Currie's traps. Let's go home, ladies. 'Tis mortal cold."

Abigail shook her head. "There may be something we can do. Follow me."

Betty suppressed a groan as the ever-energetic Abigail hitched up her skirts and petticoats and began to climb over the fence. Rachel followed and then Betty. They stumbled across a ploughed field towards a spinney at the far side. The moaning was louder now. "That is not an animal," said Abigail. "That is a man."

They hurried into the spinney and stopped short at the side of Harry Devers, sitting on the ground and clutching a bloody head.

"Mr. Devers!" cried Abigail. "You are hurt." She thought quickly. Their home was much nearer than Mannerling. "Betty, run home and fetch Barry and the carriage. We will convey him home and send for the physician!"

Harry Devers looked up at the twins, at first thinking he was seeing double. They were dressed alike—same gowns, same bonnets, same fair hair and blue eyes.

He groaned again. "Hush," said Abigail, kneeling down beside him. "Help is on the way."

"My cursed horse." He looked about him.

"Probably gone back to the stables," said Rachel. She took off her shawl and wrapped it about him. "You must keep warm. No, do not try to move."

But Harry tried to stand up, put his hand to his head, and fell back unconscious again.

They helplessly slapped his hands and rubbed them, praying all the time that Barry would arrive.

When they heard the rumble of carriage wheels from the road, Abigail ran out of the spinney crying, "Over here, Barry. Come quickly."

Barry had called at the farm first and came across the fields with farmer Currie and two of his men. They were carrying an old door on which they placed the unconscious body of Harry. Then he was laid in the carriage while farmer Currie said that he himself would ride to Mannerling and tell Mr. and Mrs. Devers what had happened to their son while one of his men had already been sent to fetch the physician.

How the girls wished that Miss Trumble were still with them as they clustered outside the bedroom door, talking in hushed whispers while the physician examined Harry.

At last he emerged and smiled at the anxious faces. "A severe concussion. He must not be moved. I will call tomorrow to see how he goes on."

Betty darted up the stairs to whisper that Mr. and Mrs. Devers had arrived.

Lady Beverley was all that was gracious. She explained they would consider it an honour to look after their son while the girls wished again Miss Trumble were here to deal with this odd situation. How should they behave towards a man who had so cruelly assaulted their sister?

"It is most kind of you," said Mrs. Devers with a break in her voice. "We are deeply in your debt. After the way Harry behaved . . . But no matter. You will all have an opportunity to find out how much he has changed."

Barry, listening at the door, decided to ride over to Hursley Park as soon as he could get away and warn Miss Trumble of what was happening. The combination of the heir to Mannerling and the Beverley sisters was far too dangerous!

But when he arrived at Hursley Park that evening, it was to learn with dismay that Lord Burfield had invited Lady Evans and Miss Trumble to join him while the Makepeaces were his guests. Lord Burfield had realized that an invitation to the Makepeaces might be misconstrued, and as he had not yet made up his mind to propose to Prudence, there was safety in numbers, and so apart from Lady Evans and Miss Trumble, he had invited other people as well. Barry secured Lord Burfield's address and returned home to write a letter, putting aside some money out of his savings so that he could send an express to Miss Trumble on the following day.

But on the next day snow, which had fallen during the night, was lying in drifts on the roads, and more snow was falling. He could not get to Hedgefield to meet the mail coach, the Deverses could not even get over from Mannerling to see their son, nor could the physician call. It was left to the Beverley sisters to nurse Harry Devers back to health.

He recovered quite quickly and proved a surprisingly docile patient. Rachel was the first to thaw towards him. Finding her alone with him one day, Harry apologized most humbly for his treatment of Jessica.

Rachel gave a little shiver and said, "I think it is all to do with Mannerling. I think that house drives everyone who has anything to do with it a little mad."

But Harry, looking at her golden hair gleaming in the candle-light, and at her soft pretty manners and gentle face, was already beginning to plot. He had vowed to get even with the Beverleys, but that would not answer. In order to restore his good name and get out of the army, the solution would be to marry one of them, and who better than Rachel? She was not like her sisters. She was gentle and kind and would make a compliant wife. He would go carefully this time. No grabbing or kissing until after the wedding.

And so it was mostly Rachel who read and talked to Harry. The bedroom door was always open and the servants always about, and Harry was always so grateful and cheerful that they all began to think he was really reformed. It was their Christian duty to forgive the sinner, they firmly believed that, and there was no sensible Miss Trumble around to warn them that rakes did not reform; only their mother, who was becoming increasingly excited at the progressing friendship between Rachel and Harry.

Rachel's one weakness was that she had too high an opinion of her own common sense. She was not in love with Harry, and felt sure that all her old desire to regain Mannerling had gone. But she did not want to remain a spinster. That was a truly dreadful fate. Harry was pleasant and kind and truly reformed. They were friends. She would have her own household. Now that Miss Trumble had gone, Rachel found that she longed to get away from her mother with her petty miserliness and erratic changes of mood.

Had Harry returned to drinking anything at all stronger than lemonade, he might have betrayed his real nature, but he was enjoying playing the part of saint. He could get well and truly drunk on his wedding day, but not before.

There was a sudden brief thaw, which allowed Mr. and Mrs. Devers to visit their son and find him recovered enough to return home with them.

They had feared for his life and so, when he humbly begged them to give him permission to marry Rachel Beverley, they felt he had indeed become the son they had always longed him to be. Marriage to one of the Beverleys would restore his good name. Lady Beverley was approached and cried tears of joy. She thought only of returning "home."

Rachel was surprised and amazed at Harry's proposal. Somehow she had not talked much about him with her twin. Abigail was always telling her she was too soft-hearted, and so Rachel had thought that any remarks in Harry's favour would be met with scorn. But when she prettily and gratefully accepted Harry's proposal and Harry had driven off to Mannerling with his parents, she was taken aback by her sisters' dismay.

They gathered in her room, and Belinda was the first to speak. "You must not sacrifice yourself, Rachel," she said. "None of us cares a rap for Mannerling any more."

"I am not sacrificing myself," said Rachel. "I truly like Mr. Harry, and we deal together extremely well."

"I should not have left you alone with him so much," mourned Abigail. "Send Barry immediately with a letter to say you made a mistake. Do that, Rachel, before an announcement is made in the newspapers."

"But I do not want to cry off," said Rachel, still bewildered by their reaction. "I thought you would all be happy for me."

"Miss Trumble will be shocked when she learns of this," said Lizzie. "It never would have happened had she been here."

"Miss Trumble is a lady of good sense. She will see with her own eyes how Harry has changed," said Rachel. "I will insist Mama invite her to the wedding."

Unaware of the bombshell about to be dropped on her by the announcement in the *Morning Post*, Miss Trumble had settled quietly into Lord Burfield's house party. She had accepted in her mind that Lord Burfield—so suitable for poor Abigail—was shortly about to propose to Prudence Makepeace, whom

Miss Trumble damned in her mind as a sly, devious, and yet tedious girl.

But Lord Burfield still hesitated. He was plagued with memories of Abigail Beverley's bright hair. He reminded himself he had done the sensible thing and then wondered immediately afterwards why doing the sensible thing should fill his days with such restless boredom.

Prudence had studied the subjects dear to his heart as diligently as she could, but as she did not have Abigail's quick mind, she merely repeated to him, parrot fashion, whole paragraphs out of books, and as Lord Burfield had read some of the same books, he could only marvel at her memory and begin to wonder if she had one original thought in her head. He began to picture what their married life would really be like. Would she quote books to him at the breakfast table? Or, having secured him, would she stop making any effort to please him?

Miss Trumble, although she often thought of the sisters and wondered how they were faring, was enjoying being away from the burden of daily worrying about them. Lady Beverley had treated her just like any other servant, and that had rankled. It was pleasant to be in a richly appointed household with every comfort. There was plenty to read, and interesting walks to take when the snow cleared a little more.

When she had first arrived at Lord Burfield's home, Miss Trumble had waited eagerly every day until he had finished reading the morning papers so that she could read the news, but as each easygoing day followed its leisurely pace, she lost interest in the news, and that morning would not have troubled him for them had he not handed the newspapers to her.

She read all the news—about the hard winter, about how the Thames was frozen over, and about the war. Idly she turned to the social column of the *Morning Post*.

Miss Trumble stared down at the announcement of the forthcoming wedding between Harry Devers and Rachel Beverley with horror. Her first impulse was to beg the use of the carriage and travel directly to Brookfield House. But on calmer reflection she realized there was nothing she could do. She had been dismissed. To tell any of the Beverleys to cancel a wedding which meant giving up their hopes of Mannerling would be useless. And to think she had firmly believed all that obsession was over. But Rachel, gentle Rachel and Harry!

When Lady Evans entered the morning-room, Miss Trumble pointed to that terrible announcement.

"So one of your chicks has done well for herself," remarked Lady Evans.

"What can you mean, dear lady? Harry Devers is a libertine, a rake, and half mad."

"Well, that's the gentlemen for you, Letitia. They are all the same," said Lady Evans, which led Miss Trumble to wonder feverishly what on earth the late Lord Evans had been like.

"On the other hand," went on Lady Evans, looking at the anguish in her friend's eyes, "if you think you can do something, by all means take my carriage and go to Brookfield House."

"You are very kind, but believe me, Lady Beverley will be in such ecstasies at the thought of regaining Mannerling, not to mention having secured a rich son-in-law, that I doubt if she would even let me across the threshold."

"You must not become too exercised over this,"

said Lady Evans. "You know how it goes in marriage—a few nasty experiences and a few children and then the husband is ever absent in his clubs or on the hunting field and the lady is left alone to her own pursuits. It is the way of the world. Ah, good morning again, Rupert. I am trying to reassure Miss Trumble. She is distressed because one of her recent charges has become engaged to Harry Devers of Mannerling."

Lord Burfield sat down and looked inquiringly at Miss Trumble. "Which one?" he asked.

"Rachel Beverley," said Miss Trumble.

He felt a sensation of relief. "Ah, Miss Abigail's twin. So what is so terrible about this Harry Devers? Oh, I remember the gossip. He was engaged to another Beverley and she jilted him after he assaulted her. The Beverleys must be desperate for husbands. Or could it be that they are merely desperate to get Mannerling back and will go to any lengths to achieve that aim?"

"I suppose so," said Miss Trumble. "Oh, but it is so hard to believe! You have met my girls, Lord Burfield. Are they not as clever as they are beautiful?"

"Indeed they are, Miss Trumble. But perhaps the mother is behind all this. I must say I took her in dislike, in such dislike, in fact, that it ruined my memories of a very pleasant evening."

Miss Trumble's eyes were suddenly shrewd. And ruined your interest in Abigail, she thought.

A letter from Barry arrived a few days later. It was not the sort of letter Barry would have written had he been able to get to the mail coach sooner. In it he said he had at first been shocked and dismayed and had ridden to Hursley Park to find her gone. But he said that, hard to believe though it might be, Harry

Devers was behaving like the veriest gentleman and perhaps the softness and goodness of Rachel had reformed him.

"He's lost his wits as well," muttered Miss Trumble.

Harry Devers rode off to rejoin his regiment after Christmas. He whistled and sang, stopping at the first posting-house of the road to get very drunk indeed. He had much to celebrate. His parents had promised him that he could leave the army and settle at Mannerling as soon as he was safely married.

The wedding was to be held at Mannerling the following April. Lady Beverley was opening the purse-strings wide. She had even taken Rachel to London to have her fitted for her wedding gown.

Abigail felt she should not worry about this marriage so much. Rachel was calm and placid. She had explained to Abigail that she and Harry dealt well together and she was not interested any more in regaining Mannerling but merely in getting married and having a home of her own. And yet, several times Harry had mistaken Abigail for Rachel and Abigail felt that he should have been able to tell the difference. Lizzie and Belinda were also uneasy. They were all frequent visitors to Mannerling, but the great house seemed unable to cast any of the old spell on them. Only Lady Beverley seemed rejuvenated. She was grander and haughtier than ever, and the poor squire who had been so kind to them after their ruin, supplying them with fish and game, and arranging entertainments for them, was accorded only a brief nod from her ladyship when she saw him in Hedgefield.

It had been a hard winter, with snowy days and bitter frosts, so that for a long while time seemed to stand still. But at the end of February a skittish warm spring wind blew across the bare fields and the sun shone down, reminding them all that the wedding would soon be upon them.

Rachel's gentle insistence that Miss Trumble be invited was first met with scorn, but it was Mrs. Devers, who was so anxious to restore her son's good character in the eyes of the county, who changed her mind. Mrs. Devers suggested it would be politic to invite Lady Evans to the wedding, so why not Miss Trumble as well? Lady Evans, on receiving the invitation decided to call on Mrs. Devers, taking Miss Trumble with her.

Mrs. Devers was all that was gracious. To Lady Evans's protest that she was getting too old for such events, Mrs. Devers pressed her to stay for the wedding at Mannerling as her house guest, pointing out that Lady Evans would therefore not have to make even the short journey home. Lady Evans pointed out that at the time of the wedding, she would have a house guest, Lord Burfield. Mrs. Devers insisted that Lord Burfield should be invited as well. As the Deverses were putting up most of the money for the wedding celebrations, Mrs. Devers felt she could include anyone she liked in the wedding invitations, without first consulting Lady Beverley. Lady Evans was about to demur, but Miss Trumble said quickly, "How very kind. I am sure we would be delighted to accept."

"I am doing this only for you, Letitia," grumbled Lady Evans. "You are so eager to go to reassure yourself that one of your beloved girls is going to be happy after all. I also believe you have your eye on Burfield. It will not serve. I am most shocked that he did not propose to poor Prudence. She was all that was suitable."

"What on earth was suitable about that tedious girl?" asked Miss Trumble.

"Her fortune and her family. Nothing else is of any concern in marriage."

"Mrs. Devers was most insistent that Harry had changed, but I cannot believe it."

Lady Evans sighed. "You always were too high a stickler, Letitia. Would you have us all spinsters?"

"We will see," replied Miss Trumble obscurely.

The Mannerling carriage arrived a week before the wedding to convey the Beverley family to Mannerling, where they were to stay until the great event. Buoyed up by the cheerfulness of Rachel, the other sisters were beginning to believe that, this time, the "curse of Mannerling," as Lizzie dubbed it, would not strike again.

The great house seemed to spread out its wings to them as the carriage bowled up through the formal gardens in the pale spring sunlight. Daffodils and crocuses shone on the grass. Servants were bustling about and a great red-and-white-striped marquee was being erected on the lawn, where the tenants of Mannerling would be entertained.

Rachel was delighted to learn that Miss Trumble was to be among the guests. Harry was due to return the following day. Abigail wondered how her mother had managed to afford all the expense, although she knew that Mr. and Mrs. Devers were paying for the wedding itself. All of them had new gowns, and Rachel's wedding gown was a miracle of white lace, silver embroidery, and seed-pearls. As the bride-to-be, Rachel had been allocated one of the biggest guestrooms. The first evening saw them all at dinner at Mannerling, a happy party.

When Rachel awoke the next morning, she began to feel nervous. Harry was due home and she had not really thought much about him when he had been away. She had thought only of the wedding, of her pretty gown, of having her family all about her. It was nothing to do with Mannerling, and yet there had been a little feeling of triumph inside her that she had succeeded where her sisters had failed. Now that she was back at Mannerling, she felt as if she had never left the place. She belonged. If only that belonging was not to be spoiled by having to marry Harry Devers.

She heard the sound of carriage wheels on the drive and went to the window and looked down. Harry Devers had come home. He had grown a splendid pair of side-whiskers, that much she could see. Then he took off his hat and looked up. Rachel drew back behind the curtains. Harry did not look like the handsome, fair-haired man she had last seen. His hair was thick with bear's-grease, making it look darker, and his face was swollen and red.

I must make him shave off those whiskers, she thought. He looks like a stranger. She felt she should run down and welcome him but put off the moment. She would see him at dinner that evening. She went for a walk in the gardens that afternoon with her sisters, trying to appear as cheerful and happy as she had been before seeing Harry. But Abigail was not deceived. After the walk she followed Rachel into her room and asked abruptly, "What is wrong?"

"Nothing," retorted Rachel defensively. Then she said with a reluctant little laugh, "Oh, well, a touch of bride nerves, I assume. Harry is back. I saw him from the window and barely recognized him. He is sprouting a pair of whiskers."

Abigail sat down in a chair by the window and removed her bonnet. "Perhaps you should go and see him now, Rachel, and not wait until this evening."

"I am sure he has much to tell his mother and father," said Rachel. "I will wait until dinner."

When the sisters entered the drawing-room that evening, Harry stepped forward, seized Abigail's hand and kissed it, saying, "You look more beautiful than ever, my love."

Abigail extricated her hand. "Wrong lady," she said. "You mean my sister, Rachel."

"Eh, what? Oh, yes," said Harry. "Fact is, you both look so alike, I find it hard to tell you apart."

Wishful thinking before his arrival had begun to persuade the Beverley sisters that Harry really loved Rachel and was a reformed character. They had forgotten that it was hardly a loverlike trait to be unable to tell the twins apart. Abigail could not help noticing those bristling side-whiskers, the flushed face, and the thickened body. Nor could she fail to remark that when they all sat down to dinner, that only lemonade and seltzer were being served.

"What is this?" demanded Harry loudly, staring at the jugs. "A children's party? Where's the wine, demme?"

"A word with you, my son," said Mr. Devers.

He drew Harry out of the room and said in a savage whisper, "You will drink nothing stronger than lemonade until after the wedding. Do I make myself clear? The cellars are locked and bolted until then. If you want me to buy you out of the army, you will think on that!"

They returned to the dinner table. Harry threw everyone a weak smile. He tried to maintain an easy flow of conversation during dinner but gradually relapsed into a sulky silence.

We are not having wine because his parents are frightened he will get drunk, thought Abigail in alarm. They are frightened he will betray himself.

Fortunately for Rachel, the old magic of Mannerling gripped a sober Harry. During the next few days, he was as she remembered. He took her out driving, he walked with her in the grounds, and although she often found his conversation boring, she was reassured. Everything would be all right. Husbands were not expected to be witty.

Two days before the wedding, the guests who were to stay began to arrive, among them Lady Evans, Miss Trumble, and Lord Burfield.

Lizzie could not help noticing the way Lord Burfield went straight up to Abigail, bowed over her hand, and said, "It is a pleasure to meet you again, Miss Abigail." Such as Lord Burfield, thought Lizzie, would never mistake one twin for the other.

Lord Burfield drew Abigail aside that afternoon and said, "Will you walk in the gardens with me, Miss Abigail?"

Abigail nodded her assent. Once outside, she gave a little sigh, glad to be away from the mixture of worry and pity in Miss Trumble's eyes, and the preening of her mother, who was already ordering the servants about as if she, and not Mrs. Devers, were mistress of Mannerling.

"So how does it feel to be back, Miss Abigail?" asked Lord Burfield.

"It feels as if we had never left," said Abigail reluctantly.

"And you approve of this wedding?"

"Rachel is happy."

"Is she so much in love?"

"That I do not know. But she is happy." *Was* happy, mocked a treacherous little voice in Abigail's brain. "I am glad to see Miss Trumble again," she said, "although I have not yet had much chance to talk to her."

Nor tried very hard, thought Lord Burfield, who had noticed the way the sisters had avoided Miss Trumble.

"I feel Miss Trumble does not approve of this marriage," said Lord Burfield. "There was some great scandal about Harry Devers and one of your sisters, was there not?"

"That was in the past," said Abigail. "We must always forgive, and he seemed genuinely to have reformed."

"And yet your Miss Trumble would be the first to point out that rakes never reform."

"Miss Trumble, may I remind you, is a spinster and can hardly be said to be an authority on marriage."

"That lady is very shrewd." Lord Burfield fell silent, wondering if he might after all have proposed to Prudence had it not been for the cynical look in Miss Trumble's eyes when Prudence rattled off at great speed another paragraph from the books she had studied to please him.

"Never mind Miss Trumble." Abigail quickened her pace, her cheeks pink. "It will be a very grand wedding, and everyone will enjoy themselves."

"Where do they travel for their honeymoon?"

"They are staying at Mannerling. Mr. and Mrs. Devers are to travel to stay with friends in Brighton and so leave the couple to start their married life."

"When does Harry plan to rejoin his regiment?"

"I gather he is to sell out."

"And be master of Mannerling? What of his parents?"

"I heard something to the effect that Mr. and Mrs. Devers plan to find a property for themselves and leave Mannerling to Harry. They do not like it here. Mrs. Devers says it is haunted."

"And do you believe that?"

Abigail laughed. "I have not seen any ghost since I have been here. Mr. Judd is said to walk the passages. He was the owner who hanged himself from the great chandelier in the hall."

"And does he moan and rattle his chains?"

"Nothing like that. The servants sometimes see him on a moonlit night at the end of the Long Gallery, and Mrs. Devers swore that the chandelier still turns and tinkles as if his body were hanging from it."

"Ah, here is the estimable Miss Trumble come to join us," he said. "I shall leave you."

"No, don't . . ." Abigail started to say, but he had already bowed and was striding away from her across the lawns.

"A fine man, that," said Miss Trumble, coming up to Abigail.

"Do not lecture me on Rachel's wedding," said Abigail sharply. "I could not bear a jaw-me-dead on this sunny day."

"And why should you think I would not approve?" asked Miss Trumble mildly.

"Oh, I thought you would blame poor Rachel for

marrying Harry only to regain Mannerling, but she is genuinely fond of him."

To Abigail's surprise, Miss Trumble merely smiled and said, "Well, we will see. Tell me, what have you heard from Isabella and Jessica?"

Relieved, Abigail began to tell her the news, and as they walked together in the gardens like old friends, she began to relax. Miss Trumble was back with them, however briefly, and nothing could go wrong.

Rachel, too, was relieved to receive later only polite felicitations from her old governess, not knowing that Miss Trumble had decided, with the wedding so imminent, there was nothing she could do but pray.

But that evening, Rachel could not sleep. The weather was still holding fine and it was a clear, balmy night. She looked out of the window. The garden lay silver under the moon. She had a sudden desire to go out of doors and walk by herself under the moonlight.

She got dressed and made her way quietly along the long passage outside her room which was lit by shafts of moonlight.

As she made her way down the stairs to the main landing which overlooked the hall, she suddenly stopped. The air was full of a tinkling sound. Slowly she walked on down and then stopped, her hand to her mouth. Although here was no draught, no breath of air, the great chandelier was turning, one half turn one way, then one half turn another. So must it have swung when the dead body of Judd was suspended from it.

She let out a stifled cry of fear and turned and ran headlong back to her room. She undressed quickly and climbed into bed and pulled the covers over

her head tightly in case that sinister tinkling sound
of the turning chandelier should reach her frightened ears.

# Chapter Four

*Holy Deadlock*
— SIR ALAN PATRICK HERBERT

𝒯wo THINGS HAPPENED the following day—the day before the wedding—to set a train of disastrous happenings in motion.

The first was that Rachel, after a restless night, looked feminine and vulnerable, the very thing to quicken Harry's lecherous senses. The other was that a bottle of brandy appeared on his bedside table.

John, one of the footmen, who had worked for the Beverleys when they were at Mannerling, and had been rude and insolent from the moment he learned of their ruin, had felt sure that Rachel would find a way to have him dismissed as soon as possible after the wedding.

There seemed no doubt that the wedding would take place, as Harry was acting the perfect gentleman and the cellars had been locked up and all the servants had been told not to allow him anything strong to drink.

And so John had ridden into Hedgefield and bought that bottle of brandy and slipped into Harry's room and placed it tenderly on the bedside table.

Harry was convinced that he only needed a few bracers to make him feel comfortable. But somehow he had drunk most of the bottle without really noticing anything other than the warm glow in his stomach. He decided to go downstairs and entertain the company. It was unfortunate that he met Rachel, on her own, also making her way downstairs. Her light muslin gown fluttered around her slim body, the low neckline showing the swell of her breasts. There were shadows under her eyes, making them look enormous.

"A word with you, sweeting," said Harry. He took her arm and propelled her into the nearest room, which happened to be the one that had been allocated to Miss Trumble.

"My sisters are waiting for me," said Rachel nervously.

"It occurs to me," said Harry, leering at her, "that I haven't even had a kiss to welcome me home."

Rachel looked at him doubtfully but then decided a kiss was in order. She closed her eyes and puckered up her lips.

He gave a coarse laugh and jerked her into his arms. He forced his mouth down on hers. He reeked suffocatingly of brandy. His grasping, groping hands were going everywhere that innocent Rachel had never believed a man's hands could go. Maddened and made strong with fear, she wrenched herself out of his arms, ran out the door and down the passage to her own room. Harry shrugged. After tomorrow, he wouldn't need to behave himself. He went back to finish the brandy.

Abigail and the others finally went in search of Rachel when she did not put in an appearance. They found her lying on her bed weeping, a handkerchief held to her mouth.

"Come now," said Abigail, alarmed. "What is this?"

"It is Harry," said Rachel in a choked voice. "I cannot marry him."

"What has he done?" asked Belinda.

"He kissed me and he stank of brandy and it was disgusting. I hate him. I cannot go through with the wedding."

The sisters looked at one another in alarm. It was as if the house reached out to them again, demanding their loyalty, demanding their return.

They clustered around Rachel on the bed, trying to find out what it was Harry had done that was so very terrible. A brandy-soaked kiss? All men drank.

"His hands were everywhere," said Rachel, modesty stopping her from describing where his hands had been.

Lizzie said, "I will fetch Miss Trumble."

"No!" cried Belinda and Abigail in unison. They were back in the grip of their obsession with Mannerling. They had been home again.

Rachel dried her eyes and sat up in bed. Her face was very white. "That is that. I must see Mama. I cannot marry Harry Devers."

"Oh, I could have handled him," said Abigail.

"Then *you* marry him!" Rachel flashed out. The twins, both angry now, glared at each other, one looking like the mirror image of the other.

Abigail suddenly gave a little laugh. "Why not?"

"But he won't turn round and propose to you," wailed Lizzie. "Anther rejection. If he does not kill Rachel, it will be a wonder."

Abigail waved an impatient hand for silence. "The day may yet be saved. Have you noticed how many times Harry has mistaken me for you, Rachel?"

Belinda stared at Abigail in amazement. "Are you

thinking of taking Rachel's place? It would not answer. Mama—"

"Mama," interrupted Abigail scornfully, "is the last to notice the difference."

"Miss Trumble," said Lizzie.

"Ah, yes." Abigail rose to her feet and began to pace up and down the room. "Let me think. For a start, you were not going to wear a veil with your wedding gown, Rachel, for everyone thinks veils are quite exploded. But I shall wear that veil. Then, if you act a little bolder, Rachel, and I become meeker, and wear your clothes, and you wear mine, we will pass muster. Miss Trumble will not be expecting me to marry Harry and so she will think it is you."

"There is Lord Burfield," said Lizzie in a worried voice. "He always knows it's you, Abigail."

"But again, he will not be expecting the switch. Nobody would think us capable of such a monstrous idea."

Rachel gazed at her twin, wondering what to do. She knew she could not marry Harry. Abigail was the strong one. Abigail could cope with him; Abigail could cope with anyone. She, Rachel, would need to live out the rest of her life as Abigail, but that would be no bad thing. Harry had said to her that he had no intention of allowing Lady Beverley to live at Mannerling, and Rachel knew that once her mother became aware of that fact, she would retreat back into her accounts' books and fictitious illnesses.

They discussed the matter, backwards and forwards, for two hours, until the dinner bell sounded.

"It would be better not to be seen together this evening, Rachel," urged Abigail. "I will say you, Abigail, are feeling tired and you are having a meal on a tray in your room. I will go downstairs in your clothes as you. If my act fails, then we will know the game is up."

And somehow the plot, which had seem so outrageous when Abigail had first suggested it, seemed to be the only solution. Abigail's room was next to Rachel's and they shared a sitting-room, and so it was easy to change belongings from one room to the other without being observed by the servants.

Abigail sent a message by a footman that she did not require the services of a lady's-maid and dressed herself in one of Rachel's gowns, glad in a way that their new gowns were different, so that she could look more like Rachel. She even smoothed a tiny bit of lampblack under each eye to imitate the shadows under her sister's.

Harry, having had nothing more to drink, and having slept heavily, was sobered enough to regret his behaviour. He should have held off until after the wedding. It was therefore with great relief that he found himself joined in the drawing-room before dinner by a shy "Rachel" who actually flirted with him modestly and prettily. Abigail was in luck. Lord Burfield was spending the evening with friends in Hedgefield and Miss Trumble was keeping to her room. Lady Beverley, as usual, was acting out the part of mistress of Mannerling and did not notice anything odd.

As Harry made every effort to please, Abigail became more and more convinced that she was doing the right thing. Once the marriage was a few months old, she would tell Harry the truth and they could be married properly, in secret. With the beautiful rooms of Mannerling surrounding her, Abigail felt she could achieve anything.

Before she retired that night, Abigail went to her

twin's room to tell her that everything would be all right.

"There is something you must do," said Rachel, her eyes wide and dark in the candle-light of her room. "You must somehow not consummate the marriage until Harry knows who you are and agrees to a proper wedding. For if he flies into a passion, you must be able to annul the marriage."

"I have heard ladies talk about asking gentlemen to wait," said Abigail. "That is what I shall do. He seemed most eager to please. Are you sure you were not frightened over nothing?"

Rachel gave a shudder. "No, and I hope you know what you are doing, Abigail."

"I will manage. Remember, tomorrow you will have Miss Trumble watching you, so try to behave as much like me as possible. But as one of my bridesmaids, she will not see you until we march up to the altar in the Yellow Saloon and so your back will be to her during the service. If she suspects anything is wrong after I am married, then she would not dare say anything because of the disgrace."

Rachel clutched her arm. "Listen, Abigail. Last night I could not sleep. I decided to go outdoors, but when I got as far as the landing, the main landing, the chandelier was turning and tinkling, backwards and forwards, although there was no wind, just as it must have done when Judd's body was hanging from it. It is an omen."

"Pish! You are overset and so you imagined it all."

"No, no, I feel something bad is going to happen."

"All will be well. Mannerling will be ours again. The ladies can always manage the gentlemen if they are of strong enough character."

"But Jessica was very strong and yet Harry shocked her and almost made her ill with fright. And her dress was torn."

Abigail could feel all her confidence beginning to ebb away. "Jessica was already in love with Mr. Sommerville and . . . and . . . she had just turned Harry down, and that is enough to make any gentleman mad with rage." She determinedly talked on about the rightness of what they were about to do. Had they been men, then the world would have applauded them for fighting to regain their home and estates. Rachel listened, feeling guilty, but at the same time feeling so relieved that she would never, ever have to face the ordeal of becoming Mrs. Harry Devers.

The next day, Rachel determinedly bounced about, trying to look sure and confident. Abigail was bathed and dressed by the maids and then, when she was ready, her mother came to see her. Lady Beverley was as short-sighted as she was vain and would never wear spectacles for anything other than poring over her precious accounts, and so she saw only the daughter she assumed was Rachel.

"You are very lucky, my child," said Lady Beverley, "that you have brought us all home again."

"As to that," said Abigail, remembering what Rachel had said, "I fear that Harry does not wish you or my sisters to live at Mannerling."

"You must be mistaken!" exclaimed Lady Beverley. "You are too young to run such a mansion. You will need guidance."

"He was most firm on that point," said Abigail,

suddenly realizing that a distressed mother would not pay too much attention to her.

"Oh, you must have misunderstood him," said Lady Beverley. "I will speak to him." And to Abigail's relief, she hurried from the room.

Abigail was glad she was not to be married in church. Had that been the case, she could not have gone through with it. But there would be nothing particularly sacrilegious about tricking everyone, just for a little, in a house wedding.

Miss Trumble sat in one of the little gilt rout chairs in the Yellow Saloon among the other guests and awaited the arrival of the bride. Her heart was heavy and she felt old. Looking after the Beverley sisters, teaching them, had given her a purpose in life. She could only pray that Rachel would find Harry reformed, and if she did not, then would have the sense to leave him.

Mr. Stoddart, the vicar, stood before the temporary altar. There was a rustling among the guests. Harry was standing before the vicar with a fellow officer as brideman. Then the double doors were thrown open. Abigail, veiled, walked slowly in on the arm of the squire, who had forgiven Lady Beverley all her recent snubs and had agreed to give Rachel away. Behind her, pretty as a bouquet in white muslin and wreaths of silk flowers in their hair, came Rachel, Belinda, and Lizzie

Lord Burfield looked sharply at the bridesmaids. Then he looked at the bride. He could only see their backs, and yet he had the oddest feeling he was seeing Abigail being wed and not Rachel.

Lady Beverley cried most affectingly during the

service. Harry had confirmed her fears. He did not want her at Mannerling.

The long service dragged on. Miss Trumble was glad when it was over. The deed was done. It was up to Rachel now. The bride raised her veil and turned around.

Miss Trumble drew in a sharp breath. Surely the bride was Abigail, and that bridesmaid was Rachel! But then she shook her head. The twins would not dare to play such a monstrous trick. As if aware of her gaze, Abigail modestly dropped her eyes.

Lord Burfield stared at the bride with a puzzled expression on his face. But like Miss Trumble, he could not believe for a moment that anyone would play such a monstrous trick. During the festivities, he took Rachel up for a dance, believing her to be Abigail. He found her unusually quiet. When they were promenading after the dance, he said, "You seem remarkably subdued on such a happy occasion, Miss Abigail."

"It is sad to lose my twin," said Rachel.

"You are both remarkably alike, are you not? Your own mother must often mistake the one of you for the other."

"Yes, she does. But her eyesight is not very good."

"I shall be in London for the Season. Is there any chance that you might be there?"

Rachel shook her head. "We do not go to London."

"And you would like to go."

It was not a question. Lord Burfield was remembering how Abigail had told him about her boring life in the country. But Rachel did not know that and said quietly, "I enjoy life in the country. There is much to interest me."

Again he experienced that puzzled feeling of unease.

He did not find himself elated and charmed in her company as he had been before. Rachel's next partner came up to claim her and he saw the relief on her face.

The long festivities went on. The bride and groom went out to the marquee on the lawn, where Harry, who was becoming increasingly tipsy, made a muddled speech to the tenants.

Abigail, who had been congratulating herself on how well she was playing her part and in her mind's eye was already making several alterations to the furnishings of Mannerling, was taken aback when Harry said, "It is time for us to retire."

"So soon?" Abigail looked at him wide-eyed. "But our guests are still here."

"They will know we want to be alone. Come along."

Abigail allowed him to lead her upstairs. She turned on the landing and looked down. Lord Burfield was gazing up at her. She felt trapped in that blue gaze. Then Harry jerked her arm impatiently and she turned away.

He followed her into her room and stood staring at her lecherously, rocking a little on his heels.

"If you will leave me for a moment," said Abigail, "I will ring for the maid."

He advanced on her. "I will be your maid."

Abigail smiled weakly. She was his wife now. She could hardly push him away. But she tried to play for time. Perhaps if she got him to leave her for a short while and go to his own quarters, he might fall asleep.

"I have a vastly pretty night-gown," she said flirtatiously. "I hoped to surprise you."

To her relief, he laughed and said, "Very well. But I will be back very soon."

Once he had gone, Abigail undressed, washed, and put on a silk night-gown trimmed with fine lace. She climbed into bed and lay staring up at the canopy, listening to the sounds of merriment filtering up from below. Gradually it dawned on her that what she had hoped for had actually happened. Harry must have fallen asleep.

One by one, carriages began to rumble off down the drive. Voices could be heard raised in farewell.

At last, she closed her eyes and composed herself for sleep. That was when the door crashed open.

Harry, wearing a brightly coloured dressing-gown, strode in. "You should have sent for me," he grumbled. A branch of candles was still burning brightly on a table at the window. Harry took off his dressing-gown, revealing he was naked underneath. Abigail let out a whimper of fright and crouched back against the pillows. He climbed into bed and fell on top of her, his mouth, hot and wet and reeking of stale drink, covering her own in a suffocating embrace. With a superhuman effort, Abigail broke free and ran for the door.

"Hey, come back here!" he roared.

Abigail jerked open the door and fled along the passage. She shot round a corner. She heard him thudding after her. She opened the nearest door, slipped inside, ran for the bed, jumped in and pulled the covers over her head and lay trembling.

And then she heard the striking of flint on tinder-box and the room was bathed in the soft light of an oil-lamp. Beside her in the bed was Lord Burfield, looking down at her quizzically.

"Is this an old-fashioned country way of celebrating a wedding?" he asked.

"Demme, where the deuce is that hell-cat?" came a yell from the passage.

Frightened out of her wits, Abigail clutched Lord Burfield by the shoulders. "Do not betray me," she begged.

"You're Abigail!" said Lord Burfield. "I knew there was something strange. You married Devers, not Rachel, and yet your name was given as Rachel."

"Rachel couldn't bear it," said Abigail, "so I took her place."

"WHAT!"

The door crashed open. Harry Devers stood there, his dressing-gown clutched about him. Behind him stood Lady Beverley, Miss Trumble, and Lady Evans.

Abigail squeaked with terror and threw her arms around Lord Burfield's neck.

"I'll kill you, Rachel," said Harry.

"This is not Rachel," said Lord Burfield. "It's Abigail."

Lady Beverley began to scream hysterically, great rending screams which sounded through the rooms and passages of Mannerling, screams which roused the roosting peacocks outside and set them screaming in a mad imitation.

"I knew it," said Miss Trumble bleakly when Lady Beverley's hysterics had subsided into hiccuping sobs. "A curse on this house!"

A council of war was held in the drawing-room, the other interested house guests being kept away.

Harry and Abigail were now dressed, as was everyone else there: Mr. and Mrs. Devers, Harry, the Beverley sisters and their mother, Lord Burfield, Miss Trumble, and Lady Evans.

"Before you all begin shouting at each other again,"

said old Lady Evans, "we had best begin at the beginning. Rachel!"

Rachel said in a low voice, "I could not go through with it and so Abigail said she would take my place. I knew Harry did not love me and so I knew he would not notice the difference. He often mistook Abigail for me."

"You are wicked, wicked girls," said Mrs. Devers. "Only look at my poor boy!"

Harry Devers hung his head. His brain had been working at a furious rate. The Beverleys were shamed, shamed beyond repair. Nobody would believe Jessica's story now. Now *he* was the victim. If he did not rant or rail, but looked totally crushed by the shame of it all, his parents might still allow him to sell out and stay at Mannerling without the encumbrance of a wife. If he shouted and stamped, then sympathy might veer in Abigail and Rachel's direction, and he wanted them to suffer as much as possible.

"This is what comes of having got rid of Miss Trumble here," said Lady Evans. "Had she still been in your employ, Lady Beverley, none of this would have happened."

"We have come to the conclusion," said Mr. Devers heavily, "that Harry here has been more sinned against than sinning. I think he has had a lucky escape. There is quite obviously madness in the Beverley family."

"How dare you!" said Lady Beverley, but her protest sounded weak.

"I do not think we should bear the expense of a wedding which never took place," went on Mr. Devers. "A wedding at which our son was so deeply hurt and shamed, too. So I am going to send you a bill for the expense, Lady Beverley."

This, for Lady Beverley, was the final straw. She fainted dead away. Maids and footmen came running. The lady was restored to consciousness and then helped to her room.

"I would be grateful," went on Mr. Devers, "if you girls would take yourselves off and never set foot in this house again. As for you, Abigail Beverley, not only did you trick my poor son most shamefully but you were discovered in another man's bed with your arms around his neck."

And Lord Burfield found himself saying, as he looked at Abigail's wretched face, "As to that, Miss Abigail and I will be married soon enough, and that should lay that particular scandal to rest."

Everyone stared at him.

"Yes, that is a very good idea," said Miss Trumble suddenly and decisively. "I shall go to see Lady Beverley immediately, Lord Burfield."

He bowed and she hurried from the room.

"I cannot . . ." began Abigail, but he said, "Later, we will discuss this later. Go home and I will call on you. Go and pack, and my carriage will be waiting for you."

Rachel, desperate to get out of the room, tugged at her twin's arm.

When the sisters had packed and their luggage had been carried out to Lord Burfield's carriage, a shaking Lady Beverley was then supported out to it by Miss Trumble. "I am coming back with you," said Miss Trumble. "Get in."

It was a silent journey home, broken only by the muffled sobs of Lady Beverley.

When they arrived at Brookfield House, Barry came running out in the dawn light to meet them.

His face broke into a glad smile when he saw Miss

Trumble, but the smile faded as he saw Rachel and her sisters descend from the carriage as well. "Rouse the maids, Barry," said Miss Trumble crisply. "You girls, get to bed immediately, except for you, Abigail. I shall see you in the parlour as soon as I have settled Lady Beverley."

Abigail felt almost numb with shame and disgrace. Out there, like the dawning light, she knew the full enormity of what she had done was waiting to strike her with force. She sat down wearily in the parlour and removed her stylish bonnet, a dashing shako, put it on her lap and stared at it. It was a reminder of all her mother had spent on Rachel's wardrobe so that she would be a bride worthy of Mannerling. Mannerling. The curse of the Beverleys.

She wanted to stay numb. The minute she started to "thaw," she knew she would begin to cry, to cry without stopping. How mature and confident she had felt only the day before. Now she felt young and childish and lost.

Barry came in and made up the fire. He turned to leave and looked as if he would like to say something, but at that moment the door opened and Miss Trumble came in. Barry nodded to her and left.

Miss Trumble sat down opposite Abigail and studied her gravely. "I am not going to berate you on your folly," she said. "I am here to talk sense to you about Lord Burfield. He is a fine man, a gentleman in the true sense of the word, and he is prepared to marry you."

Abigail found her voice. "He cannot," she said. "He will always feel he has been coerced into marriage, and he will never forgive me."

"My child, you were already so deep in disgrace

that he could easily have walked off and forgotten about you and no one would have blamed him. Why were you in his bed?"

"I was running away from Harry. I ran into the first room. I was so frightened, I did not hesitate to see whether the room was occupied or not. I had regarded him as a friend. But I cannot marry him."

"Did anything happen between you and Harry? Are you still a virgin?"

"Yes, I am still a virgin."

"Faith, I begin to feel sorry for the dreadful Harry."

"I cannot marry Lord Burfield," said Abigail again.

"There is nothing else you can do. After the way you have behaved, no other man will ever want you. I do not know what will become of your poor sisters now. Go to bed and sleep as best you can. When Lord Burfield calls I suggest you accept prettily and be suitably grateful. I have spoken to Lady Beverley of this. If you turn Lord Burfield down you will be left here in Brookfield House with a very embittered mother."

Abigail stared at her. Then the full impact of her monstrous behavior finally struck her. She began to cry, her shoulders shaking, tears streaming down her face. She stood up to leave. Miss Trumble stood up as well and then moved forward and put her arms about the sobbing girl. She said nothing, merely held Abigail until the girl finally grew calmer. "Go, now," said Miss Trumble quietly, "I will be staying. Try to get some sleep. I will awake you when Lord Burfield arrives."

Miss Trumble felt weary. She decided to have a few hours sleep herself. Her bags had been carried up to her old room. But before she retired, she decided to have a word with Barry. He had not gone back to bed but was out in the stable, talking to the horse, a habit he had when he was upset. "Oh, miss," he cried when he saw her. "What happened?"

Miss Trumble sat down on a bale of hay and looked up at him. "Rachel felt she could not go through with the wedding. By that time, the girls were back in the grip of Mannerling, and so Abigail took her place."

"Oh, fan me, ye winds!"

"Quite. Abigail had some mad idea perhaps that she could get Harry to marry her properly, for she was wed under Rachel's name, and all would be well. But her introduction to the marriage bed, fortunately for her only the introduction, scared her witless and she ran straight into Lord Burfield's bed, where she was discovered wrapped around him."

"Ruin and damnation. This will be a household of spinsters, shunned by all."

"There is one bright spot on the horizon, Barry. Lord Burfield is to call this day to make a formal proposal of marriage to Abigail."

Barry looked at her doubtfully. "A gentlemanly thing to do, but he will make a most reluctant bridegroom."

"I think not. I think he is much taken with Abigail. It was not his fault that she threw herself into his bed. He had no reason to do anything at all."

"But what will become of the others?"

"We will see. Now I think I should get a little sleep."

"Are you home again, miss?"

Miss Trumble gave a wry little smile. "Yes, home again."

Abigail awoke when Miss Trumble shook her by the shoulder. "Lord Burfield is called," said Miss Trumble. "Rouse yourself. Betty is here to help you dress. Choose one of Rachel's prettiest gowns. You may as well adopt her trousseau."

"I cannot face him," said Abigail.

"Don't be silly. Up with you."

Abigail climbed out of bed and allowed herself to be washed and dressed.

Her golden curls were brushed until they shone. In a gown of blue muslin with three flounces at the hem and with a white muslin pelisse over it, she was finally declared fit to descend and meet her suitor. "Your mama is resting," said Miss Trumble. "I will leave you alone with Lord Burfield for ten minutes."

"Oh, do not leave me," cried Abigail. "I do not want to be alone with him."

"Don't be silly. This is not Harry Devers, this is a gentleman." She gave the reluctant Abigail a little push into the parlour and then left.

Lord Burfield looked down at Abigail, who stood before him, her head hanging.

She found her voice, which came out in a sort of rusty whisper. "I am so sorry. You need not do this."

"I am well aware of it. But it might serve very well. I want a wife and I am weary of looking for one; you need to restore your reputation. Please be seated and hear what I have to propose."

Abigail sat down. There was a great black weight of misery in her stomach.

"You and your family will travel to London, to my house in Park Street. My aunt, Mrs. Brochard, will be in residence. We will be married quietly by special license. We will go about socially and you and your sisters will look beautiful, radiant, and confident. The scandal will have reached London before us, but you will receive many invitations from the curious. If I am right, sooner or later Harry Devers will disgrace himself in such a way as to restore your good name. At the moment, even I can find it in my heart to be sorry for him."

"You are being coerced into marriage," said Abigail.

"Not I. As far as the intimacies of the marriage bed are concerned, that must be your choice. You must come to me. In the near future, we will get to know each other better."

Abigail sat for a moment in silence. Then the full generosity of his offer struck her. They would all be in London, with places to see and theatres to visit instead of sitting, hiding in the country, scorned by all.

"I accept," she said in a small voice.

"I thought you might. Now let us get Miss Trumble in here, as your mother appears to be too indisposed to see me."

He rang for the maid and sent her to fetch the governess. Miss Trumble listened to his plan. She felt quite lightheaded with relief. It was far more than any of the Beverleys deserved.

"Perhaps you will convey this intelligence to Lady Beverley," said Lord Burfield, rising and picking up his hat and gloves from a side-table. "I will send my travelling-carriage for you next Wednesday and a fourgon for the servants and your luggage."

Miss Trumble curtsied low.

After he had left, she lectured Abigail on the extent of her good fortune and then went to order the carriage and Barry to take her to Hursley Park.

* * *

In all her relief, the normally shrewd Miss Trumble had not quite realized the full horror at Abigail's behaviour that Lady Evans felt. Nor had she realized quite how much Lady Evans had dearly wanted to make a match between Prudence Makepeace and Lord Burfield. Miss Trumble told her old friend everything, including the plan to defer the intimacies of the marriage bed until such time as the couple came to know each other better.

Lady Evan's lined and autocratic face stared wrathfully at Miss Trumble from under the shadow of one of her enormous starched caps. "I fail to see, Letitia," she said, "why a lady like you of breeding and intelligence should be acting as servant to a parcel of whores!"

"That is going too far!" cried Miss Trumble.

"Whores," repeated Lady Evans firmly. "What else are they? To connive and plot and trick and deceive, and all for gain. Prudence Makepeace would have made him an excellent wife."

"Why?" demanded Miss Trumble crossly. "She is sly and devious and worse—boring!"

"She has modesty, breeding, and a fortune. Riches always marry riches in our world. I can only hope that Rupert does not consummate the marriage. It can then be annulled as soon as he realizes the enormous mistake he has made."

Miss Trumble drew on her gloves. "They are good girls at heart. I promised little Lizzie that I would stay with them until she was married."

"That's the youngest? The odd creature with *red* hair and *no* dowry to speak of? Dear heavens, Letitia, you will be with that wretched family until such time as you are carried out of Brookfield House in your coffin."

"I have great hopes of Lizzie," said Miss Trumble, rising to her feet.

"Pah!" said Lady Evans. "Pah and pooh to you, Letitia. You are as mad as the Beverleys!"

When Miss Trumble had left, Lady Evans went to her writing desk and began to pen a long letter to Mrs. Makepeace, describing all the details about the forthcoming wedding between Lord Burfield and Abigail, ending with, "The only hope is that the wedding will be annulled as soon as he realizes his great mistake, for he does not plan to enter into proper marital relations at first."

The letter was sanded and sealed and sent express and delivered to Mrs. Makepeace by the post boy the following day. Prudence listened carefully as her mother read the letter aloud. She sat with her head bowed, shredding a fine cambric handkerchief between her fingers. It just wasn't fair. How had she failed? For she could not blame Abigail for having coerced him into marriage and therefore spoiling her own, Prudence's, chances. Lord Burfield had not declared himself during her visit to his home. In fact, during the latter part of her visit, he had seemed to go out of his way to avoid her.

But just suppose . . . just suppose, so ran her busy mind, that he realized his mistake quite soon and she would be there at the Season, there on hand to highlight the difference between her own fortune and ladylike behaviour and that of the dreadful Abigail Beverley. He would surely find out how society shunned this new fiancée of his. She did not voice any of her plans aloud. She meant to have Lord Burfield, and Abigail Beverley was not going to stand in her way.

"Are you coming to London with us, Barry?" asked Lizzie two days later. She was sitting in the tack-room, watching Barry polishing the harness. Barry put down the cleaning-rag. "I do believe so, miss. We are all going with the exception of Josiah, the cook, and two of the maids, who will keep the house fired here. Never does in these wicked times to leave a house unattended."

"But who will look after the garden when we are away? It is most odd of Mama to take you as well when you are so badly needed here."

"The decision was Miss Trumble's, your poor mama having withdrawn into herself, so to speak, and not caring about anything."

"And why does Miss Trumble want you in London?"

"I reckon it's because I told Miss Trumble I had never been there and it was a lifelong dream to see the place. Miss Trumble is a very kind lady."

"I am glad she is back with us," said Lizzie. "But London will be hard for us, Barry. Everyone will jeer and sneer, you know—there go the terrible Beverleys."

"Lord Burfield does seem a mighty strong and powerful man, miss, and I would reckon he knows what he is doing."

There was a silence and then Lizzie said in a small voice, "What is the news from Mannerling?"

"Not good, Miss Lizzie, and that's a fact. They do say that Mr. Harry is gone into a decline, what with the shame of it all."

Lizzie paled. "What if he dies and Abigail is blamed for it?"

"Now, then," said Barry comfortably, "I did not mean to alarm you. See, to my way of thinking, Mr. Harry is so keen to get out of the army and stay at Mannerling that he will pull every trick in the book. I do not believe for a moment that one is really ill."

Harry sat at the toilet-table in his bedroom and carefully applied another layer of white lead cosmetic to his face. He then extracted a little lampblack and applied interesting dark circles under his eyes.

He practised a few groans and, satisfied with the effect, he climbed back into bed, pulled the *Sporting Life* from under his pillows where he had hidden it, and settled back for an enjoyable read.

After a few moments, he heard someone approaching. He thrust the paper under his pillow and uttered a few of those well-rehearsed groans. His father and mother came into the room and stood at the end of his bed, looking at him with worry etched on their faces.

"I have news for you, son," said his father in a low voice. "Although the wedding did not take place, it is clear to me that you are unfit to return to the army because of the way you have been humiliated. To that end, I agree to your selling out. You may remain here quietly until such time as, God willing, your health is restored."

"Thank you, Papa," said Harry in a weak and trembling voice.

"We will leave you now. Try to sleep."

As soon as they had left, Harry got out of bed and performed a victory dance on the floor. Mannerling was his! No more army. He would try to keep up the pretence of illness and mental ruin for as long as he could. Then he would be free to be lord and master of all he surveyed. That would mean getting his parents to move out. But he felt Machiavellian. He could handle anything!

# Chapter Five

*I'm not a jealous woman, but I can't see*
*what he sees in her,*
*I can't see what he sees in her, I can't see*
*what he sees in her.*
— SIR ALAN PATRICK HERBERT

BELINDA CONFIDED TO Lizzie in a hushed whisper that she could not help feeling excited at the forthcoming visit to London. Lizzie murmured back, "It does feel wicked to be looking forward to it so much, what with Mama confined to her room with another of her mysterious illnesses and Rachel and Abigail red-eyed with weeping. But it will be so wonderful to escape from here and the shadow of disgrace."

"It's a shadow that will follow us to London," warned Belinda.

"Oh, I know that. But we will be going *out*! Not sitting indoors mourning the Beverleys' lost reputation. And Miss Trumble says that we must behave like perfect little ladies so that society will begin to remember Harry's awful reputation and not think too hardly of Abigail. But I am so glad Miss Trumble is with us again," said Lizzie.

"So am I. She is now so cheerful and reassuring, and keeps talking of how pleasant it will be to have a box at the opera again. I asked her when she had ever had a box at the opera, and how could a governess manage to be accepted by the opera committee to even have a box because, as you know, they are worse than the patronesses of Almack's."

"To which Miss Trumble no doubt said that it was a previous employer who had the box," said Lizzie.

"Exactly."

"There is a mystery about our Miss Trumble. Companions are usually bullied just like governesses, and yet Lady Evans treated her with every respect, quite like an old friend. A number of governesses actually come from very good families who have fallen on hard times," said Lizzie.

"That must be the case," agreed Belinda. "But I am a little disappointed. I wanted the mystery about Miss Trumble to turn out to be something really dramatic."

"I cannot imagine anything at all dramatic in our sober Miss Trumble's past," said Lizzie. "We have not really discussed this Lord Burfield, and yet I had some conversation with him at Lady Evans's ball."

"You did not tell me that!"

"I felt it was something I was supposed to keep a secret and yet I suppose I can tell you, now that he is to be our brother-in-law and has behaved most handsomely. I was sitting in a corner at the ball and Prudence Makepeace, a not-so-young lady, was sitting with him. When his attention was distracted, I saw this Prudence slip something into his glass. Well, I was afraid to make a scene but frightened she might have been trying to poison him, so I switched the glasses!"

"Lizzie!"

"She staggered off shortly after having drunk what was in the glass. Lord Burfield went to find out what had happened and it turned out to have been laudanum. I think she wanted to stop him calling on Abigail!"

"This Prudence will no doubt be furious then when she learns of Abigail's marriage."

"I doubt if we shall see her again," said Lizzie. "We shall be in London, and this Prudence will no doubt be somewhere in the country. She is too old to expect another Season."

"How old?"

"Oh, middle twenties, something ancient like that."

"I hope I never get to be that old without being wed," said Belinda.

Abigail and Rachel went out for a walk the day before their departure for London. Both had eyes red with constant weeping. Abigail now could not think of any way to justify her mad behaviour. Rachel felt her twin's shame and yet took comfort from the fact that she had not had to marry the dreadful Harry.

"How could I have been so naïve about him?" mourned Rachel, not for the first time.

"It was wishful thinking," said Abigail sadly, a tear spilling down her cheek. "He seemed such a reformed character and we were all so willing to believe he would make you a suitable husband and that Jessica had exaggerated. I did not know until yesterday that Jessica had refused to attend the wedding. Mama kept that from us, saying that Jessica was ill and that Isabella was unable to travel from Ireland. There was a letter this morning from Jessica to Miss Trumble. I did not ask her what was in it, for I am sure it would be full of recriminations."

"Pooh, Jessica made the same mistake herself," said Rachel. "We have not talked of Lord Burfield, Abigail."

"He is kind, but I am frightened that he, too, will turn out to be some sort of monster. I wish we knew more about gentlemen."

"No one could be as bad as Harry Devers," said Rachel fervently. "Barry says he is still keeping to his bed, but says he is probably trying to coerce his parents into buying him out of the army, and in the meantime making our shame worse by acting the part of the broken man."

"I seem to have lost my courage," said Abigail in a low voice. "I was always so confident and felt so strong. It will not be at all difficult for me to behave well in London. I do not think I will ever again feel anything other than meek and crushed."

Rachel kicked at a grass turf moodily with her half-boot. "And yet," she said slowly, "are we entirely to blame? Harry played his part so well and Mr. and Mrs. Devers played theirs. We are young and naïve. Despite Miss Trumble's excellent teaching, we have been trained to believe that our only mission in life is to find husbands. Even Miss Trumble is determined that we should marry. And just look how society damns spinsters, calling them ape-leaders and worse."

"If only I were rich," sighed Abigail, "then I could thank Lord Burfield for his generous offer and refuse him."

"I do not think you have ever looked at him clearly," said Rachel, giving her twin a sidelong look. "He is very handsome, intelligent, and amusing."

"I agree. But I feel nothing more for him than friendship."

"I believe that is more than any miss in these wicked days can expect. Oh, well, perhaps things will not be too bad in London. We are to stay with Mrs.

Brochard, Lord Burfield's aunt, until you are wed. I do hope she is a pleasant lady and does not disapprove of us too much."

"I do not think she can, or she would have refused to have anything to do with us," said Abigail. "Miss Trumble says she does not plan to go out with us socially very much and so we will certainly need someone other than Mama to chaperone us. I think Mama is going to retreat into her imaginary illnesses for quite some time."

Mrs. Brochard was a thin little French lady who had come to England after the French Revolution, or, as it was still known, the Bourgeois Uprising. Apart from her black eyes and dyed black hair and elegance of dress, there was nothing very French about her. Her accents were those of the English ruling class and she did not even lard her conversation with French phrases, as was fashionable in society. She had accepted her nephew's, Lord Burfield's, offer to chaperone his fiancée and her family until his wedding for one reason only: to see if she could sabotage this most unsuitable alliance.

Having only the sparse information that Abigail Beverley was good *ton* and intelligent, Mrs. Brochard immediately got her spies out to learn more and found out all about that disastrous wedding at Mannerling.

To this practical, hard-headed, and unemotional Frenchwoman, who had never been softened by any love, either for her late husband or for any of her ten children, eight of whom had died before the age of five years, it all seemed very straightforward. Abigail had not chosen her nephew's bedroom by accident. She had deliberately set out to entrap him. Mrs. Brochard also found out that there seemed to be so little of a dowry that it was practically negligible, and that confirmed her worst fears. She dug further and learned all about the Beverley obsession with their old home. At first she had sat down to pen a strong letter to her nephew telling him that she would have nothing to do with such a disgraceful family. But then she tore up the letter and with long, thin, beringed fingers dropped the scraps on the floor and sucked the end of her quill. Rupert of course would know every circumstance of the Beverleys and he was no fool, and yet he still wanted to marry this Abigail. So the poor man must be besotted. Opposition to the marriage would mean that he would simply find another chaperone for these disgraceful girls.

No, she must entertain them and appear pleasant on the surface and plot underneath.

Lord Burfield arrived to take up residence. Awaiting the arrival of the Beverleys, Mrs. Brochard received a card from a Mr., Mrs., and Miss Makepeace, her butler saying they were asking for Lord Burfield.

Mrs. Brochard tapped the card thoughtfully. She could send a message downstairs to say Lord Burfield was at his club. She knew *of* the Makepeaces, of course. She knew about everyone in society. The daughter was a great heiress. "Send them up," she commanded her butler.

Mrs. Brochard adjusted her lace cap in the mirror and straightened her damask gown before turning to the door with a smile of welcome on her rouged lips.

When the Makepeaces entered, she said effusively, "Lord Burfield is at his club, but any friends of my nephew must be friends of mine. Welcome." She rang the bell. "Tea? Wine?" They accepted the offer of tea.

When tea was served and the customary chit-chat about the Season was dealt with, Mrs. Brochard said, "You are close friends of Burfield?"

"We had the pleasure of being guests at his home," said Mrs. Makepeace. She heaved a little sigh and Prudence dabbed at one dry eye with a wisp of handkerchief.

"Your daughter is a diamond of the first water," remarked Mrs. Brochard, her eyes sharpening. " 'Tis a wonder some gentleman has not snapped her up."

"Prudence was engaged but her fiancé was killed," said Mrs. Makepeace. "Recently, we did think we had found the perfect match for her ... but, alas, it was not to be."

"Was it Burfield you intended for your daughter?" asked Mrs. Brochard bluntly.

"We did think there was an interest there, and when he invited us to his home ... But now he has been ensnared—oh, I do beg your pardon, Mrs. Brochard, I meant affianced, of course—to Abigail Beverley, my poor little Prudence must look elsewhere."

Mrs. Brochard was interested in money. The fortunes of society rattled through her brain like the beads on an abacus, until she stopped short at one bright bead which stood for Makepeace. The money came from coal mines in Yorkshire, she remembered, but that could hardly be classified as trade, as many of the aristocracy enriched themselves from coal on their lands. This Prudence was attractive and genteel. She felt a renewed burst of fury against the conniving Beverleys, but she said mildly, "I am expecting the arrival of the Beverley family soon and will be chaperoning them until the wedding. I would do anything for my nephew, you understand, although I believe that family is in deep disgrace. You know the scandal?"

The Makepeaces nodded sorrowfully.

"It would be vulgar of me to discuss Burfield's affairs. All I will say is he is not married *yet*!" And they all smiled at each other like conspirators.

After they had left, Mrs. Brochard went out to call on various society ladies, and at each house she bemoaned the fact that she had to chaperone such disreputable girls. "Burfield thinks they will restore their good names when society sees them," she said with a sigh. "But what member of society is going to stoop to entertain such a parcel of adventurers?"

And so various ladies of the *ton*, who had been considering inviting the Beverley sisters out of sheer curiosity, now mentally cancelled those invitations.

John, the footman at Mannerling, learned through the newspapers of Abigail's engagement. The newspapers had been kept from Harry, so John made sure he got them, along with a regular supply of brandy. He also informed Harry that the Beverleys had gone to London and were being chaperoned by Lord Burfield's aunt, Mrs. Brochard.

Harry listened to all this with a blank look of boredom, but as soon as the footman had left, he hurled the newspapers across the room in a fury. He was not going to let them get away with it. They should never be forgiven. They should all be ostracized for the rest of their days and go to their graves spinsters. But what could he do about it, confined to his room as he was, playing the invalid? He became determined to find a way of going up to London himself and spiking their guns. He was attended daily by the physician, a cunning old Scotchman who was quite prepared to humour the foibles of the rich. He knew Harry was not ill with anything other than an occasional overdose of brandy.

So Harry suggested to him in a faint voice that perhaps he should rally and go to London for the Season, that such diversions as the Season had to offer might restore him. And when he suggested that the physician, Mr. Sinclair, should accompany him, Mr. Sinclair was all too ready to agree to the idea of a paid holiday in London.

"It is like a riding accident, don't you see, dear lady," he said to Mrs. Devers after his consultation with Harry. "Your puir boy has been crossed in love. Were he to find a suitable lassie at the Season, it waud stabilize him wonderfully." And so worried were Mr. and Mrs. Devers about the mental condition of their son that they readily agreed to open up the town house in London.

Harry rubbed his hands. Every ball, every party Abigail attended, he would be there. He would cry brokenly when he saw her and that would damn her further than she had already been damned. It should be brought home to Burfield the shame he was bringing on his name by marrying a Beverley.

Lord Burfield had equally doting parents. He had called on the Earl and Countess of Drezby on his road to London to tell them of his forthcoming marriage, saying the reason for the speed was because he was very much in love. They were delighted for him, gave him their blessing, and said they would travel up to London to meet the bride-to-be and to attend the wedding. It was after he had left that they received a letter from Mrs. Brochard, the countess's sister, outlining succinctly why their son was marrying Abigail Beverley and how he had been entrapped. They were at their wit's end as to what to do. Rupert, Lord Burfield, had inherited his present home and estates from a great-uncle. Threatening to disinherit him would not stop him from committing this folly. But they had to try. They ordered their travelling-carriage to be made ready. They would reason with their beloved son and make him see sense.

Feeling more cheerful than they had done for some time, the Beverley sisters arrived at Lord Burfield's town house. Mrs. Brochard welcomed them effusively, although she was privately taken aback by the incredible beauty of the girls. Fickle society forgave beauties much folly. She was also nonplussed by the mien and appearance of their governess. Although the Beverleys were quickly put at ease by their welcome, although Lady Beverley immediately complained of feeling ill due to the rigours of her journey and retired to her room, this Miss Trumble had a sharp look in her eyes and Mrs. Brochard had an odd idea that her welcome had not deceived the governess one little bit. In fact, Miss Trumble seemed more like the head of the family than Lady Beverley and asked Mrs. Brochard if she had successfully "nursed the ground," that is, secured invitations to the polite world for her charges.

"It is very difficult," complained Mrs. Brochard. "I have done my best, but you must realize, Miss Trouble—"

"Trumble."

". . . Trumble, that the circumstances of Miss Abigail's marriage have already reached London and no one is willing to invite anyone with such a shocking reputation." There was a little gleam of triumph in her eyes as she said this.

"Tell me," said Miss Trumble, "what is the next most important social event?"

"The Duchess of Hadshire's ball. But the invitations have been out this age and the duchess is a high stickler."

"And when does this ball take place?"

"Next Wednesday, in a week's time. Forgive me for pointing this out, but you have an authoritative air which does not befit a mere governess, Miss Trumble."

"Oh, I beg to disagree," said Miss Trumble placidly. She rose and curtsied and left the room.

Miss Trumble arrived at the Duchess of Hadshire's later that day in a hack. She stood outside for a moment and then took a rather worn card out of her reticule, a visiting card she had not used for some time.

She knocked loudly at the door. The butler who answered it raised his eyebrows in supercilious surprise to see an elderly lady without any maid or footman demanding an audience with his mistress. "I am afraid her grace is not at home," he said. The door began to close.

"Give her grace my card," said Miss Trumble, edging into the space still left in the doorway. "I assure you, she will be most upset should she learn I had been turned away."

The butler hesitated a moment. Miss Trumble's air was haughty. He inclined his head. "Be so good as to wait here." He would have left her on the step, but with surprising energy Miss Trumble pushed past him, walked to a chair in the hall and sat down.

He ascended to the drawing-room, his back stiff with disapproval. In a few minutes he returned, his manner totally changed. He bowed low. "Be so good as to follow me."

Gathering up her skirts, Miss Trumble followed him upstairs into a light, pretty drawing-room. The Duchess of Hadshire ran towards her, both hands outstretched. "Letitia," she cried. "I thought you were dead." The duchess was a still-pretty woman in her late thirties. She wore a flowered muslin gown and a lace cap as delicate as a cobweb on her brown hair. Her odd sherry-coloured eyes gazed on Miss Trumble with affection. "Where have you been? No one has heard of you this age."

So Miss Trumble began to talk while the duchess listened wide-eyed. When Miss Trumble had finished, she said, "You always were a rebel. Do you remember that gentleman I was so determined to marry and you would have none of it and you introduced me to my dear duke? I owe you a great deal. So you wish an invitation to my ball for the dreadful Beverleys. Of course you shall have the invitations. Mrs. Brochard will be furious, of course."

"Why? I cannot go about in society, as you know, and she is supposed to be chaperoning them."

"Mrs. Brochard called on me to bewail the fact that no member of society of any breeding would ever dream of entertaining the Beverleys. As I had not intended to ask them, I did not pay her much heed, but I gather she has been busy trying to ensure that everyone knows of the scandal. She does not approve of the engagement."

"I thought as much," said Miss Trumble. "Yes,

there is a very great favour I wish to ask of you, Harriet . . . I wish you to make a call . . ."

"So you say," Lord Burfield was exclaiming, "that you have not managed to secure even one invitation for the ladies?"

The Beverley sisters, Lord Burfield, and Mrs. Brochard were taking tea in his town house.

"Alas, it is so difficult," mourned Mrs. Brochard. "I am afraid the scandal about that wedding at Mannerling reached London before you." She spread her thin hands in a Gallic gesture. "I am afraid no one wants to entertain them."

Abigail hung her head.

Lord Burfield felt a surge of anger. What a two-faced lot they were in society, always gleefully looking for something to be shocked about. It was a world in which ladies sent cuttings of their pubic hair to Lord Byron and where married ladies entertained lovers, and yet all delighted in the humiliation of a virgin.

Then the drawing-door opened and Miss Trumble walked in with the Duchess of Hadshire. "We met on the doorstep," said Miss Trumble. "I once worked for her grace's mother. Her grace is one of my former pupils."

She made the introductions and sent a servant to rouse Lady Beverley. Hearing that a duchess was in the drawing-room was enough to make Lady Beverley forget she was supposed to be ill. She hurried to join the company, thankful that she had been already dressed and lying on a day-bed in her room when she received the news of the duchess's arrival.

The duchess was maliciously amused by the consternation in the eyes of Mrs. Brochard. Then she surveyed the dreadful Beverleys with interest. They were outstandingly beautiful. She could understand why the twins had been able to fool Harry Devers at the wedding. They were looking-glass twins, although Abigail appeared the stronger character. Lady Beverley came in looking remarkably well for a lady who only that morning had been claiming to be at death's door.

After tea had been served, the duchess, with every appearance of enjoyment, dropped her bombshell. "I am come," she began, delicately setting down her teacup on a satinwood table beside her, "to beg you to forgive the lateness of these invitations and to come to my ball next Wednesday."

"We are charmed ... charmed to accept," said Lady Beverley.

"I know this is going against your wishes, Mrs. Brochard," said the duchess sweetly, "for you were most insistent when you called on me that no lady of the *ton* would dream of inviting your charges. I believe you told the same story to every other influential hostess in London."

"That cannot be true!" exclaimed Lord Burfield.

"But," went on the duchess blithely, "I realized that this is Harry Devers we are talking about, that lecher and madman, enough to drive any girl of sensibility out of her wits. So I am come to beg you to attend."

"That is most gracious of you," said Lady Beverley.

The duchess opened her reticule and laid the invitations on the table. "Now I must go," she said, rising to her feet. Everyone rose. The ladies curtsied. Lord Burfield bowed, and only Lizzie near the door saw that as the duchess passed Miss Trumble, one eyelid drooped in a mischievous wink.

There was a long silence after she had left, and then Lord Burfield said in a thin voice, "My study, I think, Aunt." He walked to the door and held it open. Mrs. Brochard swept angrily past him.

Once they were in the study, he shut the door and confronted her. "How dare you!" he demanded wrathfully. "You were supposed to restore their reputations, not sabotage them."

"The duchess is mistaken," said Mrs. Brochard. "I have been pleading with various hostesses to give them invitations."

"I only need to make a few calls to prove you are lying."

"I tried to save you from your folly!" cried Mrs. Brochard. "With all the young ladies available, did you need to choose such a hussy?"

"I will not listen to one word of criticism against Abigail Beverley."

"And there is that sweet creature, Prudence Makepeace. So rich, so suitable."

"When did you meet her?"

"She called here with her parents when you were at your club. They agree with me that you are about to make a disastrous marriage."

"Enough!" he said furiously. "Pack your bags and get out!"

After she had left, he buried his head in his hands. The fact was that he was now regretting his proposal to Abigail. She was quiet and meek and subdued and not at all the girl he had believed her to be. But he could not go back on his proposal. He had obtained a special license. There was nothing he could do but go through with it.

He roused himself to take his affianced out for a drive. She sat miserably beside him and answered

him in monosyllables. He heaved a tired little sigh.
Perhaps he should have let his aunt have full rein.

To the sisters' dismay, Miss Trumble was not to
accompany them to the ball. "I have not been
invited," she said firmly.

"But the duchess is very fond of you," said Lizzie.
"I even saw her wink at you!"

"You are mistaken," said Miss Trumble. "Duchesses
do not wink."

She kept them busy right up to the ball, practising
their dancing steps, making sure they still knew how
to walk gracefully, to hold a conversation, and to flirt
in a genteel manner.

Then the day of the ball passed in a flurry of hair-
dressing and pinning and making last-minute embell-
ishments to their toilettes.

Miss Trumble heaved a sigh of relief when she
waved goodbye to them. They were looking vastly
pretty and Abigail had recovered some of her spirits.

The duchess's town house in Grosvenor Square
was ablaze with lights. Music filtered out through
the drizzly London air. Abigail felt a lightening of
spirit. Tonight she would forget all about her shame
and present a brave face to society. Miss Trumble
had said they must not look at all downcast, no
matter what happened.

The first hour of the ball went well. All were
curious about these famous Beverleys. And then disaster struck in the form of Harry Devers. The minute
he arrived and saw Abigail waltzing in the arms of
Lord Burfield, he began to cry most bitterly. Several
men led him off to the refreshment room to drown
his sorrows. Everyone began to say, "Poor Harry.
Those Beverleys have no shame." Lord Burfield

could only dance with Abigail twice, and she and her sisters suddenly found that no one wanted to dance with them. Although Lord Burfield took Abigail in for supper, Belinda, Rachel, and Lizzie had to go in with their mother. The duchess did what she could, but the weeping Harry had gathered too much sympathy about him. Lord Burfield decided he should take them all home before their humiliation became any worse.

But after supper there was to be a performance by a famous opera singer before the dancing recommenced. Harry, fortified by brandy, took a seat in the front row for the performance so that everyone could see him.

And then, to his horror, his ex-mistress, the opera singer Maria Lani, walked onto the small temporary stage. The accompanist rippled over the introductory notes. Maria opened her splendid mouth, her magnificent bosom heaved, and then she saw Harry.

Her eyes blazed. "I cannot sing with that man in front of me," she said. "Harry Devers tried to rape me."

Harry had drunk too much brandy. He stared at her through a drunken red mist. "You whore," he shouted. "You liked it well enough. You used to moan and cry for more."

The gentlemen who had earlier so tenderly escorted him to the refreshment room now bore down on him and carried him out, kicking and screaming abuse.

Maria began to sing. Society sat in a stunned silence. The minute the recital was over, there was an excited buzz of gossip. There was Abigail Beverley, beautiful and delicate. No wonder she had fled such a satyr. She could not have coerced Burfield into marriage, for, under the circumstances, he had not needed to propose to her. And was not Burfield one of the biggest prizes on the marriage market? He could have had anyone. The tongues wagged busily. When the dancing recommenced, all the Beverley sisters had partners and Lord Burfield was able to relax.

So everything would have been comfortable from then on had not a certain Lady Tarrant approached Lord Burfield. She was his age, in her early thirties, witty, amusing with a clever jolie-laide face. Her mouth was too large and generous for beauty and her eyes too small. He had once fancied himself a little bit in love with her, but she had gone off and married old Lord Tarrant who, he remembered with a little shock, had died only the year before. She was wearing a daring dress of green gauze and Roman sandals which showed that she had painted her toe-nails gold.

"What a coil," she said by way of greeting. "I have not enjoyed myself so much this age. What an exciting life you do lead. About to marry one of the infamous Beverleys! And yet, after Devers's performance tonight, all are saying that they are more sinned against than sinning. Is it true that they would do anything at all to get their old home back?"

"You are a wicked rattle-pate," said Lord Burfield. "No, it is not true. All gossip."

But a shadow crossed his face. Once again he saw Abigail clutching the gates of Mannerling. He was a rich man. Would she, once they were married, try to get him to buy it for her? He realized he hardly knew anything about Abigail Beverley.

"Would you do me the honour of granting me this dance?" he said.

She took his arm. "No, it is the quadrille and I am tired of leaping about. Let us have something to drink and a comfortable coze."

The duchess saw them walk together to the refreshment room. Lady Tarrant said something, her eyes with their ridiculously long lashes flirting up at Lord Burfield, and saw the way he laughed and began to worry. It had been assumed that Burfield was besotted with Abigail, hence the engagement, but there had been nothing loverlike about his behaviour.

Lord Burfield could only guess later that his subsequent behaviour had been the result of too much champagne combined with a desire to escape from his forthcoming marriage. He found Lady Tarrant extremely amusing and very desirable. And so, when he thought that the refreshment room was temporarily empty, he leaned forwards and planted a kiss full on Lady Tarrant's generous mouth. Lady Tarrant kissed him back and then said with a laugh, "It is just as well I am a woman of the world, Burfield, and recognize that kiss as the act of a man suffering from wedding nerves."

But little Lizzie, tucked away in a corner of the refreshment room with a glass of lemonade, saw that kiss and felt that life was becoming worse and worse as the see-saw went up and then down. How terrible it had been when they had seen Harry arrive, and then how wonderful it had been when he had shown himself in his true colours. And now, down into the depths again. Lord Burfield was kissing a lady who was not Abigail.

Abigail meanwhile danced on, behaving so correctly that her gentlemen partners who had hoped to find a femme fatale found instead a young débutante of deadly politeness. But Abigail thought she was acquitting herself very well.

Lord Burfield was silent in the carriage home. He had asked Lady Tarrant to go driving with him and she had accepted. A rebellious little voice in his head was telling him that he deserved a little fun.

Abigail climbed sleepily into bed, feeling more comfortable than she had done for some time. Miss Trumble, who had been sitting up waiting for them, on hearing of Harry's terrible behaviour smiled with satisfaction. "Excellent. Now everyone will be fighting for an invitation to the wedding in case he turns up and makes another glorious scene."

"But it is to be a very quiet wedding, with just family present," protested Lord Burfield.

"We know that," Miss Trumble had said. "But they do not. We will be showered with invitations."

So it was all quite successful, thought Abigail, settling herself back against the pillows. Then her bedroom door opened and in the faint glow from the rushlight in its pierced canister beside the bed, Abigail made out the figure of Lizzie.

"Why, what is it, Lizzie?" she called softly.

Lizzie scampered over and jumped on the end of the bed. "I must tell you," she said breathlessly, "that I saw Lord Burfield in the refreshment room with a lady I found out later to be the widowed Lady Tarrant. He kissed her on the lips and she kissed him back."

A lump like ice began to form in Abigail's stomach. "Are you sure?"

"Oh, very sure. They did not see me. Then he

begged her to go driving with him this very afternoon and she said, 'You should be looking after your little fiancée.' And he said, pulling a mournful face, 'Too much time for that after I am shackled!' "

"Oh, dear," said Abigail. "What am I to do?"

"You should be asleep," came Miss Trumble's voice from the doorway. Lizzie flew to her, crying out all about Lord Burfield kissing Lady Tarrant and how he was to take her driving that day. It was five in the morning.

Miss Trumble lit a branch of candles and drew a chair up to the bed. "Did you ever wonder why Lord Burfield really proposed to you, Abigail?"

"Now, I do not know," said Abigail. "I thought . . . I thought it was because he was being heroic, riding to our rescue to save our reputations."

"No gentleman is that altruistic," said Miss Trumble. "I think he was fascinated by your spirit and intelligence. I have noticed that you are uncharacteristically dull, Abigail. It is possible he finds you a bore."

"Then I will release him from the engagement," cried Abigail.

"Think before you do. Here is a handsome and rich man, very attractive to the ladies, a fact which seems to have escaped you, Abigail. Before you throw up your hands and let him go, therefore creating more gossip and scandal, I think you should try to charm him. Come now, Abigail, you were always a fighter. Beauty in itself is not enough. Lady Tarrant has little, but I believe most men find her fascinating. Think about it. Come along, Lizzie. It is far too late for you to be still awake." She blew out the candles and led Lizzie from the room.

Now Abigail was fully awake. She thought and thought about Lord Burfield. She had simply treated him like a brother. He had never kissed *her*. Somehow she had to get him to kiss her, and before he went out driving with Lady Tarrant!

They had plenty of callers the next day, the men they had danced with, various London hostesses anxious to mull over the horror that was Harry Devers. Abigail joined in the entertainment of their guests but her eyes were always straying to the clock. Five o'clock was the fashionable hour to go driving. Her eyes flew to Miss Trumble for help as the hands of the clock began to move up towards five.

"The weather has turned fine," said Miss Trumble, looking out of the window. "My lord, why do you not take Miss Abigail out to the Park for a drive? She has been indoors too much."

"I am afraid that is not possible," he said. "I have a prior engagement."

"How interesting," said Miss Trumble. "What engagement is that, my lord?"

He looked across at her, a glint of anger in his blue eyes, and said evenly, "That is my business."

He stood up and bowed all around and then made his way quickly from the room. Abigail watched him go and felt the beginnings of anger. She excused herself, went to her room, and changed quickly into a carriage dress.

She went out of the house and round to the mews in time to see Lord Burfield driving off in a high-perched phaeton. But he also had a curricle, she remembered.

"So you escaped from your chains?" said Lady Tarrant, laughing as he drove her around the Park. Lord

Burfield was becoming conscious of the stares and raised eyebrows in their direction. Of course, he thought angrily, they were still all abuzz with rumour, gossip, and speculation after the ball last night. Now people might believe that Abigail had actually coerced him into marriage. He had not seen Lady Tarrant for some years. But her damped muslin gown left little to the imagination, and as her bold, flirtatious eyes turned up to his, he realized with a little shock that Lady Tarrant had probably got a certain reputation.

But there was worse to come. He suddenly became aware of the fact that he was no longer the focus of attention. Carriages were stopping, some men were standing up to get a better look.

And then, in front of his horrified gaze, Abigail Beverley drove towards him in his racing curricle, drawn by two of his most spirited horses, driving them well up to their bits. As she swept past him, she threw him a mocking smile.

"Was not that your little fiancée?" asked Lady Tarrant.

"Yes, and driving my racing curricle, and without my permission!"

"She is a superb whip. You should have no fear for your horses. I would advise you, Burfield, not to confront her or rail at her with so many fashionables watching. Let us continue our drive as if nothing is amiss."

"You must forgive me. I cannot continue to go on with any air of calm. I will take you home and then await Miss Abigail's return."

"As you will. But do not be too stiffly on your stiffs. If I am not mistaken, Miss Abigail discovered that you were taking me on a drive and now she has thrown down the gauntlet."

"I think she has run mad," he said furiously.

"Did you see that?" said Prudence Makepeace to her mother and father, and they all craned their heads to watch Abigail and then swung back to witness the angry departure of Lord Burfield.

"I do not understand," said Prudence. "That lady with Burfield did not look at all respectable. Her dress was so thin, you could see her garters."

"That was Lady Tarrant, a widow," said Mr. Makepeace. "She is good *ton*."

"I do not understand," wailed Prudence again. "I was not invited to the duchess's ball, but Hetty Dempster was and she called to crow over me and tell me all the gossip. What hope have I if he is going to court a tart as well as marry Abigail?"

Abigail drove competently into the mews. The first person she saw was Lord Burfield, standing outside the stables and slapping his leather driving gloves angrily against his thigh. He saw her and called to the grooms, who came running out to the horses' heads.

Abigail swung herself down from the curricle with a tomboyish ease.

"How dare you!" shouted Lord Burfield. "How dare you lie to my head groom and tell him you had my permission?"

"Because he would not have let me go otherwise. I am an excellent whip," said Abigail, "but most men would not believe me." Actually, she had never handled such mettlesome horses as those of Lord Burfield and was glad to be safely back in the mews, but she was not going to tell him that.

"Do not ever, *ever*, do such a thing again!" he

roared. Then he became aware of the grinning grooms and stablehands.

"Come, let me escort you back to the house," he said in a quieter voice.

"You may find my behaviour odd," snapped Abigail as she fell into step beside him, "but what of yours? To be seen so soon before your wedding driving a hussy in the Park is hardly the behaviour of a gentleman. Was that the famous Harriet Wilson?" Harriet Wilson was the best-known prostitute in London and had been dubbed the Queen of Tarts.

"The lady with me is all that is respectable. Lady Tarrant is an old friend, and you will speak of her with respect."

"So that you may kiss her again in the corners of ballrooms with a free conscience? If this is the way you mean to go on once we are married, I do beg you to be discreet. If I take a lover, believe me, no one will know of it," said Abigail blithely. Privately, she did not know what had come over her, never having been a prey to sexual jealousy before. She only knew she was suffused by anger, an anger which was banishing all her previous hangdog shame. She suddenly did not care whether he cried off. He should not have been driving in the Park with a tart.

He coloured with embarrassment and then rallied.

"I am sorry you learned of that. I was a trifle foxed."

"That was ever Harry Devers's trouble. Always about in his upper chambers. Brandy, I think."

He looked down at her glowing face and large sparkling eyes. He felt once more all the old attraction she had held for him. But some devil prompted him to say stiffly, "I do not like your impertinent manner. I trust when we are married you will behave like a lady."

"I shall follow your example, my lord," said Abigail sweetly, "and kiss gentlemen at balls. But, like you, I shall not tell you about it. And if I plan to go out driving with some disreputable gentleman, I shall not tell you about that either!"

He grasped her upper arm, stopped, and swung her round to face him. "You are to become my wife and you will behave modestly as befits your station. Do you forget what you owe me?"

Abigail's face flamed. "Oh, we are never, ever to forget that, are we? Then, my lord, I am quite happy to release you from this engagement."

He suddenly felt like a pompous fool. She looked dazzling in her anger, blue eyes sparkling, cheeks pink, bosom heaving. He startled Abigail by beginning to laugh. "What a coxcomb I did sound. Pax, my sweeting. I will drive only you in future and kiss only you. Truce?"

He smiled down at her and she felt breathless, nonplussed, and then deliriously happy. "Truce," she agreed. From an upstairs window, Miss Trumble who had been watching them as they stood in the street below, heaved a sigh of relief. Nothing could go wrong now.

But Abigail's troubles had only just begun. Trouble arrived in the form of a visit from Lord Burfield's parents, the Earl and Countess of Drezby. They were an elderly, dignified couple. They treated the Beverleys with courtesy but could not disguise the fact that they were sadly disappointed in the forthcoming marriage and worried about their son. But chaperoned by the eminently sensible Miss Trumble and on their best behaviour, Abigail and her sisters were making a good impression. Unfortunately, their mother decided to join the company. Lady Beverley was graciously patronizing. She sighed over the speed of the wedding and said that had not the couple been so obviously in love, she could not have given her permission. The countess bridled. "Indeed! I understood the reason for the haste was to restore your daughter's damaged name, Lady Beverley. *You* talk to me of objections! What of the sensibilities of this parent, who learns that her precious son is to ally his good name to that of a penniless girl who was prepared to marry a man in the place of her sister and ran into my son's bed instead! If I had my way, this marriage would never take place."

"We are not to be spoken to in such a manner," said Lady Beverley, beginning to cry. "We are the Beverleys of Mannerling!"

Miss Trumble rose swiftly to her feet and led her weeping employer from the room. There was a dreadful silence.

Abigail was the first to find her voice. "My lord, my lady," she said earnestly, "you must forgive Mama. When we lost our home, I fear it affected her wits. She has not been herself since then. . . . Believe me, if your son does not want this engagement, I can release him and so I have told him." She said the words with quiet dignity.

"That is true, Mama," said Lord Burfield. "I have no need to marry Abigail if I do not want to. You must not judge her by the behaviour of her mother, who has been extremely ill over all this and is desperately trying to act as if she is doing everyone a favour in order to restore some of her tattered dignity. Lady Beverley is much to be pitied."

"If this is what you want, Rupert," said the earl heavily, "then so be it. But I cannot say I like it one bit."

When the earl and countess had left, Abigail felt all her new-found spirits ebbing away. She was also bitterly ashamed of her mother. She went to her room to remonstrate with her but Lady Beverley barely seemed to hear her. She was sitting at her desk with sheets of figures. "Do you know," she said, after listening impatiently to her daughter's complaints, "that we are saving a considerable amount of money by staying here? I have calculated what we save on coals and candles alone! Of course it is as well it is to be a quiet wedding, just family, because if Mr. and Mrs. Devers had pressed on with their ridiculous request that I pay for that wedding that never really took place at Mannerling, I should have been in the suds."

Abigail wondered if it was possible to feel any more deep shame than she was experiencing at that moment. "Do you mean you refused to pay them?"

"Of course," said Lady Beverley, impatiently rattling the sheets of paper. "I simply sent them a letter of hand saying that they could take me to court if necessary. I knew they would not do that," she added complacently. "And while we are on the interesting subject of money, Jessica and Isabella have sent me certain sums. I expect you too to remind your husband what is due to me."

"Never!" said Abigail passionately. "Not one penny."

Lady Beverley sighed. "Then I shall just need to ask him myself. Do run along, dear. You are giving me the headache, standing glowering like that. Ladies should not glower. I never glower. It causes such unnecessary wrinkles."

Defeated Abigail retreated from the room. She wanted again to tell Lord Burfield that she did not want to marry him, but if she did not marry him, then he might fall prey to that harpy, Tarrant, and she could not bear that. It was so sad that his parents were disappointed in the forthcoming marriage, but they would come about after the wedding. Until then, she would behave like the veriest model débutante.

Alas for Abigail. The next social engagement was a breakfast at a Mrs. Dunwoody's home in Mayfair. Mrs. Trumble had not had to negotiate that invitation. Curiosity about the Beverleys was rife. Harry Devers had been disgraced. No one wanted to ask *him*. But the Makepeaces had been invited. Prudence was feeling her age. Other, younger, ladies were certainly arriving with their parents, but quite a number of them also had some suitor in tow.

And then she saw Abigail walking into the garden on the arm of Lord Burfield and jealousy caused her to feel slightly ill. Abigail had no right to look so radiant.

The breakfast, like all breakfasts, started at three in the afternoon. Food was served on long tables set in the garden, after which guests listened to a military band, which was later replaced by an orchestra. Dancing took place in a marquee erected at the side of the lawn.

Mrs. Dunwoody was a fashionable hostess with a rich and complacent husband who allowed her every extravagance. Neil Gow of Almack's had been hired to play for the dancers, and the band of a hussar regiment to entertain the guests while they ate delicious food prepared for them by Gunter's of Berkeley Square.

Mrs. Dunwoody did not believe in segregating the sexes, that is, placing the ladies on one side of the table and the gentlemen on the other. Nor did she believe in having married couples and engaged couples sitting together. As she often said to her husband, the poor things saw enough of each other as it was, a remark which Mr. Dunwoody accepted with his usual placid good humour.

And so Lord Burfield found himself seated next to Prudence Makepeace. She asked various questions about his home and tenants and lands and then said, "I believe I must congratulate you on your forthcoming marriage."

"Yes, I am to be married at last," said Lord Burfield, his eyes automatically straying to where Abigail sat at the other side of the table and towards the bottom end. Abigail was seated beside a curly-haired army captain. They were talking away with great animation. And the captain was young, about Abigail's age. Like Abigail, Lord Burfield did not recognize jealousy in himself. He began to flirt with Prudence, who flirted back with him quite outrageously. Abigail threw him a pained look and then began to sparkle for the army captain. "Who is the lady next to Burfield?" she asked him at last.

The captain put up his quizzing-glass. "Oh, that is Prudence Makepeace, a great heiress. It is rumoured that she was to marry Burfield. He invited the lady and her parents to his home. But nothing came of it." He coloured. "I beg your pardon, Miss Beverley. I had forgot. You are engaged to Burfield." The captain then remembered all the gossip about the young lady next to him and blushed even more miserably. Abigail saw his confusion and tried to chat to him as easily as she had been doing, but he answered her in monosyllables and so she turned her attention to the elderly gentleman on her other side, while fury at her fiancé burnt in her bosom.

Lizzie felt herself dwindling with misery. When the meal was over and the guests were walking in the garden, she said to Belinda, "That is Prudence Makepeace, the one Burfield is flirting with so dreadfully. It was she who tried to drug his lemonade."

"We must tell Abigail," said Belinda firmly.

"Oh, I wish Miss Trumble was here to counsel us," mourned Lizzie. "I do not think we should tell Abigail anything. She looks so furious."

"It is our duty as sisters," said Belinda. She walked over to Abigail and drew her aside and began to talk busily. Lizzie groaned inwardly.

Lord Burfield went off to fetch Prudence a glass of wine and Abigail moved in for the kill.

"Trying to drug my fiancé at Lady Evans's ball is not enough, I see," she said. "You must needs still try to get your claws into him even though he is shortly to marry me."

Had Prudence turned away disdainfully, the situation would have been diffused, but she said haughtily, "Poor Lord Burfield *has* to marry you," she jeered. "Everyone knows all about you. I pity him from the bottom of my heart."

Prudence was wearing a flowered head-dress. Abigail tugged it off, threw it on the ground and stamped on it. Prudence seized Abigail by the hair.

Abigail kicked Prudence on the shins and Lizzie let out a scream of horror and dismay as the warring pair fell onto the grass, kicking and biting and scratching. The men had formed a circle and were cheering them on, some of them already laying bets. Lord Burfield pushed them aside and forcibly separated the warring couple. "Come with me," he said to Abigail and dragged her off towards the house while Prudence manufactured a faint.

Abigail tried to pull away but Lord Burfield had her in a firm grip. He pulled her into the house, snapping at various staring servants to go about their business. He kicked open the door of a room which turned out to be a library, shoved her into it, followed her, and slammed the door behind them.

"Just what were you about, you hell-cat!" he raged.

"And what were *you* about to flirt with Prudence Makepeace? You complain about my behaviour and yet you flirt outrageously with that silly vapid female who tried to drug your drink at Lady Evans's ball!"

"She only took some laudanum. She did not try to drug my drink."

"She would have done if Lizzie had not switched your glasses."

He could not quite explain that he had been fully aware of what Prudence had tried to do and had been flattered that she would go to such lengths to make sure he would not call on the Beverleys.

He continued to attack. "You cannot accuse me of flirting when you were romancing that army captain."

"He was pleasant, he was very pleasant, but then he told me that you had intended to marry Prudence and had even invited her to your home. Besides, my captain is *young*."

"I being in my dotage?"

"Not yet, but close, very close, quite like little Miss Prudence."

"Bitch!"

Her hand seemed to move of its own volition. She slapped him full across the face and then stared up at him in horror.

He put his hands on either side of her face and, pulling her towards him, he kissed her full on the mouth. Abigail began to struggle but he held her close. That clever sensuous mouth moved against her own, softening from a punishing kiss into a long, languorous one. The surge of emotion, of passion, that gripped her stopped her struggles. Her hands, which had been beating on his shoulders, stole up round his neck instead. The military band outside was playing a waltz, the library smelt of leather, beeswax, and roses. He smelt of cologne and soap.

He drew back a little and looked down at her anxiously, remembering how terrified she had been of Harry's love-making. "I am sorry," he began, but she gazed up at him with a drowned look and drew his mouth down to hers.

At last he said huskily, "What a hell-cat you are! Your hair is all tangled and there are bits of grass on your gown."

"What should I do now?" asked Abigail. "Should I apologize?"

"I think that would be wise. Was the provocation great?"

"Very great. She said you were being forced to marry me."

"Love is a very great force, I have just discovered. That is why I must marry you."

"Oh, Rupert, kiss me again!"

# Chapter Six

*Romances paint at full length people's*
*    wooings,*
*But only give a bust of marriages:*
*For no one cares for matrimonial cooings,*
*There's nothing wrong in a connubial kiss:*
*Think you, if Laura had been Petrarch's*
*    wife,*
*He would have written sonnets all his life?*
*    —LORD BYRON*

THE NEWS OF the fight between Abigail and Prudence spread through polite society the next day like wildfire. It came eventually to the ears of Harry Devers, who was dreading every day that his parents, having learned of his latest disgrace, would arrive to send him back to the army.

Obsessively curious now about anything to do with the Beverleys, he made inquiries about this Prudence Makepeace and learned quickly that she had entertained hopes of wedding Burfield herself and considered Abigail had tricked him into marriage. He felt very alone. This Prudence could make a good ally. But he was not invited anywhere he might meet her. He secured her address and learned that she often walked with her maid to the shops in Pall Mall in the morning. He positioned himself outside her house until, three mornings after the breakfast, he saw her emerge. Hoping it

was Prudence and not some guest of the Makepeaces, he began to follow, wondering how to
approach her. As luck would have it, she stumbled
over a loose paving stone, and as he was right
behind her, he was able to grasp her elbow and
support her.

"Thank you, sir," said Prudence, dimpling prettily.

He swept off his hat and made his best bow, one
leg well back, his nose almost touching the knee of
the other. He straightened up and said, "I consider
myself honoured to be of assistance to such a beautiful lady, Miss Makepeace."

"You know me?" Prudence looked at him doubtfully.

"We have not been introduced. I am Devers of
Mannerling."

Her face hardened and she drew her skirts about
her as if to avoid contamination. "Ah, you shrink
from me!" he cried as she would have walked on.
"And yet I am the only person who feels for you, who
could help you."

Had Prudence not still been burning up with rage
against Abigail, she would have gone on her way, for
she had heard of Harry Devers's scandalous scene
with the opera singer. But she wanted to talk about
Lord Burfield to someone, anyone. Her parents had
forbidden her to mention his name, saying that she
must accept the fact that he was going to marry Abigail, and that was that. They had told Mrs. Brochard
the same thing, for that lady still entertained hopes
of "saving" her nephew.

"How can you help me?" she asked coldly.

"If we could talk without your maid hearing us . . ."

Prudence turned round. "Betty," she said to the
maid, "take yourself a few paces off, and do not tell
Mama of this or you will be dismissed."

They waited until the maid had backed away out of earshot. "How can you help me?" demanded Prudence again.

"There must be some way to stop that wedding from taking place," said Harry. He saw the look of distaste on her face and added quickly, "Ah, no, I am not revenging myself on the Beverleys. I am thinking of saving a decent man from being entrapped into a disastrous marriage. You have heard the scandal? Of course you have! But can you imagine how these Beverleys have nearly driven me to ruin?"

He proceeded to tell her a highly sanitized tale of how first Jessica had broken his heart and then Rachel. She believed him, because she wanted to. Her thirst for revenge matched his own.

"But what can we do?" she asked, and Harry suppressed a satisfied little smile. That "we" meant Prudence had decided to become his ally.

But his next statement shocked her. "We could make sure the wedding never takes place."

"How?" she asked faintly.

"All we have to do is keep Abigail Beverley out of the way on the day of the wedding. With the Beverleys' reputation, Burfield will assume she has stood him up."

"That is abduction you are suggesting. We could hang."

"This is my idea. I wish you to befriend Abigail Beverley."

"Never!"

"Only to find out her movements, get her confidence."

Prudence shook her head so vehemently that the feathers on her poke-bonnet looked as if they were about to take flight.

"I would be suspected."

"No, I do not think so. And who would suspect an eminently respectable young lady like you?" His mind worked rapidly. "I have a cottage on the outskirts of the village of Kensington. All I need to do is get her there the day of the wedding. Some ruse."

"But you can do that without my help!"

"Abigail attacked you at that breakfast because Burfield was flirting with you and she was jealous. Jealousy unsettles the mind," said Harry sententiously. "Your part would be merely to sow seeds of doubt in Abigail's mind about the faithfulness of Burfield. I have been busy and I have a little tidbit of information.

"At the Duchess of Hadshire's ball, one of the footmen, who had been hired especially for the evening to augment the staff, was about to enter the refreshment room when he saw Burfield with a certain Lady Tarrant."

"That disgraceful lady he was driving in the Park!"

"The same," said Harry, who had heard that piece of gossip as well. "Burfield kissed her full on the mouth and she kissed him back. The footman quickly withdrew and they did not see him."

"Are you sure of this?"

"This footman fell into the company of my man in a tavern and imparted the news. Now it could be that Abigail learned of this, hence the drama in the Park when she appeared driving his curricle. But if she were to be reminded of it, if you were to suggest that he had been seen in Lady Tarrant's company, something like that. Then, before the wedding, I will send her an anonymous note to say that Burfield is to be found at this cottage in Kensington with Lady Tarrant. She will go to confront them. Then we will have her."

"This is all too Gothic, too frightening," said Prudence, backing away. "Why should Abigail believe Burfield to be unfaithful to her? And all she has to do is ask him. Let me think about it."

"We must meet again," urged Harry.

"I will be here tomorrow," said Prudence slowly. She knew she should have nothing to do with him or his disgraceful scheme, but the thought of stopping that wedding was too tempting.

Prudence returned home and, once there, studied again a letter of apology she had received from Abigail Beverley. Abigail had not wanted to apologize, but had done so on the advice of Miss Trumble. Miss Trumble had pointed out that no insult or goading on the part of Prudence Makepeace justified tearing off that young lady's head-dress.

It was a pretty apology, in which Abigail said she had been overset.

Prudence wondered whether to call on Abigail. This letter gave her a good excuse. But away from Harry Devers, she felt she could not get embroiled in such a scheme.

But as ill luck would have it, that very afternoon Lord Burfield was walking back to his home from his club when he was hailed by Lady Tarrant, who was driving herself in an open carriage with her groom on the backstrap.

She hailed him and he climbed up into her carriage beside her. "I am not such a champion whip as your Abigail," said Lady Tarrant gaily. "Were you in the suds? And what is this I hear of hair-pulling at the Dunwoodys' breakfast? What an exciting life you do lead."

"I am forgiven for the one and the other matter has settled down," said Lord Burfield. "I am the luckiest of men."

She laughed. "I see the love-light in your eyes and it is not for me."

"Will you dance at my wedding?"

"Gladly."

He climbed down from the carriage and smiled up at her. She held out her hand and he kissed it. "I hope you are as fortunate as I," he said.

Prudence, passing with her mother in their carriage, saw that kiss and her heart beat hard. Why should that slut, Abigail, go proudly to her wedding, believing Burfield to be faithful?

She surprised her mother by saying, "I think, before we return home, we should call on the Beverleys."

"Never! After that disgraceful behaviour at the Dunwoodys!"

"Abigail Beverley wrote me the most charming letter of apology. It would be churlish not to accept that apology. Besides, if we are seen to be friends, then that gossip will die. I fear I was as much to blame as Miss Beverley," said Prudence piously.

Mrs. Makepeace was always easily swayed by her daughter. Prudence always managed to make all her actions seem right. So Mrs. Makepeace weakly told the driver to take them to Lord Burfield's home.

Now it was unfortunate that Miss Trumble had been sent back to the country by Lady Beverley on an errand. Lady Beverley had found she had left her best stole back at Brookfield House and she enjoyed the idea of making this uppity governess run errands for her.

So there was only Abigail, who was only too delighted to receive Prudence and her mother. Abigail was so much in love that she felt she could love everyone else in the whole wide world. Lady Beverley was having one of her "good" days and regaled Mrs. Makepeace with tales of the former glories of life at Mannerling, which gave Prudence the chance for a private little talk with Abigail.

"I thought Burfield was much to be pitied," she said in a low voice, "and that he was sacrificing himself. But it is you, not he, who are making the best of a bad situation."

"What can you mean?"

"I feel we have both been tricked by him. Firstly, he is seen kissing that shameless woman, Lady Tarrant, at the Hadshires' ball and then he takes her driving in the Park."

"She is an old friend," said Abigail stiffly.

"Of yours?"

"Of his."

"Oh, so you do understand. When I saw him kissing her again just before we got here, and in the middle of Hanover Square, too, I thought that perhaps you did not know."

"I don't believe you!" cried Abigail.

"Shhh! Mama will hear us, and you do not want to suffer any more scandal."

"I do not believe you," said Abigail again, while jealousy like bile rose up in her.

"All you have to do is ask Burfield if it is true," pointed out Prudence, and Abigail's heart sank.

Feeling she had dropped enough poison in Abigail's ear for the moment, Prudence, seeing her mother was ready to leave, rose as well.

Abigail paced the room after Prudence and her

mother had left and her mother had retired. It could not be true. Prudence was a jealous cat and she had only called to make trouble.

When Lord Burfield returned, it was to be met by a steely-eyed fiancée. He would have been in time to meet the Makepeaces had he not met an old army friend immediately after leaving Lady Tarrant.

He made to kiss her, but Abigail drew back. "Don't touch me!" she hissed.

"What is all this about?" He eyed her narrowly. "I hear the Makepeaces called. What did they want?"

"Oh, dear, dear Prudence called to tell me that you have just been see kissing Lady Tarrant in the middle of Hanover Square."

Now all Lord Burfield had to do was to tell the enraged Abigail that he had only kissed Lady Tarrant's hand, but he felt that as she was to be his wife, she should trust him. Had he not kissed her and said he loved her?

"I have no intention of explaining any of my actions to you," he said.

He saw the horror in Abigail's eyes and added quickly, "Come, my love, if we are going to deal well together as a married couple, you must trust me."

Abigail simply turned on her heel and walked from the room. Pride kept him where he was. That Abigail should listen to spiteful gossip from such as Prudence Makepeace and believe it meant she had to be taught a lesson. Had Miss Trumble been present, the matter would have resolved itself very quickly. Abigail would have confided in her and Miss Trumble would have pointed out to Lord Burfield that it was he, not Abigail, who needed to be taught a lesson, that a man who kissed a lady who was not his fiancée was a man to be easily distrusted.

But blissfully unaware of the gathering storm-clouds, Miss Trumble and Barry were travelling in the comfort of Lord Burfield's travelling-carriage, but not side by side, Barry being on the box with the coachman while Miss Trumble travelled inside. But when they stopped at a posting-house for the night, Miss Trumble asked Barry to join her for dinner in her private parlour. Barry knew it would be useless to ask the governess where she got the money for such luxuries as a private parlour in a posting-house.

"Well, Barry," said Miss Trumble with a smile, "all's well that ends well. Another love match."

"Let us hope t'other three will be as lucky," commented Barry.

"I do not think I will ever be easy in my mind while the Deverses are still at Mannerling."

Barry raised his thick grey eyebrows. "Don't think, miss that any of them will look on that Mr. Harry with anything more than a shudder."

"It's that wretched house," said Miss Trumble, dissecting a whiting with surgical precision. "I have half a mind to set fire to the place."

"Nothing we can do about that."

"Perhaps I will use this visit home to good use," said Miss Trumble thoughtfully.

"In what way?"

"I'll think of something," said the governess obscurely.

Two days later, Mrs. Devers was at first haughtily amazed to learn that the governess from Brookfield

House had called. She was about to refuse her an audience, but she had recently learned the news of Harry's latest disgrace and suddenly thought that Miss Trumble might have called with some awful new scandal. She asked the butler to show Miss Trumble up.

As Miss Trumble walked up the stairs to the drawing-room, the great chandelier in the hall began to tinkle. She stood on the first landing and stared at it. It was swinging in one half-circle and then slowly in another.

"Why is that chandelier swinging?" she said sharply to the butler's liveried back. "There is no wind."

He did not turn round. "I am sure you are mistaken," he said, walking forward and opening the double doors of the drawing-room.

Mrs. Devers rose and held out two fingers for Miss Trumble to shake. Miss Trumble appeared not to notice. She seized her hostess's whole hand and pumped it vigorously.

"Pray be seated," said Mrs. Devers. "Pray, what may we do for you?"

Miss Trumble looked about the room. She was alone with Mrs. Devers. The "we" had been royal. "I am come to offer you some advice," said the governess.

Now Mrs. Devers's face was rigid with hauteur.

"Indeed! I trust you are not going to deliver yourself of some impertinence, Miss Trumble."

"I trust not," said Miss Trumble equably. "You have no doubt heard of your son's latest . . . er . . . escapade."

Mrs. Devers reached a hand for the bell-rope. "No, stay, hear me out," said Miss Trumble. "I assure you I have only your welfare at heart."

Mrs. Devers dropped her hand.

Miss Trumble leaned forward, an earnest expression on her face. "I firmly believe," she said, "that all poor Mr. Harry's troubles have been caused by this house."

The look of hauteur left Mrs. Devers's face, to be replaced with one of fear. "Why do you say that?"

"There is something about Mannerling which begets obsession in the finest of people," said Miss Trumble, relying heavily on her belief that this doting mother would forget all Harry's bad behaviour before he ever set foot in Mannerling.

"I believe you have the right of it," said Mrs. Devers. "Harry was always a sweet boy and then a fine soldier. I believe this place to be haunted."

"I think it is." Miss Trumble lowered her voice. "I think it is possessed by a malign spirit. For the sake of your son's reputation, nay, his very sanity, I beg you to sell this place."

"I have wanted to this age," said Mrs. Devers. "But poor Harry is so devoted to the house . . ."

"A devotion which will lead to ruin." The wind had risen and howled round the house. Somewhere a door banged, and from the stable block came the howl of a dog.

"I believe you have hit on the one solution," said Mrs. Devers slowly. "We can never be happy here. I will speak to Mr. Devers when he returns from the estate."

Well satisfied with her call, Miss Trumble left. Of course she did not believe all that rubbish about malign spirits or haunted houses. An uneasy part of her mind remembered that tinkling chandelier, but she mentally shrugged it off. There must be some simple explanation. The wind must have risen without her noticing it.

Barry was waiting for her in the carriage. "Well, miss?" he asked curiously as they moved off down the drive.

"Well, Barry, I have succeeded in my mission, I think. I have just persuaded Mrs. Devers to sell Mannerling."

"Why?"

"Don't you see, that will remove Harry away from my girls' ambitions. Rotten place," said Miss Trumble, casting a savage look back at the graceful building. "I hope it stands empty and falls into rack and ruin!"

Prudence met Harry Devers two days before the wedding. "My poison worked," she said triumphantly. "They were both at the opera last night and the coldness between them was obvious for all to see. I cannot believe our luck. I was sure he would have explained everything to her!"

"You have done your part," said Harry. "Now I will do mine."

"He doesn't love me," said Abigail for what seemed to her twin like the hundredth time. "That whore Tarrant was at the opera and she gave him *such* a look. And he has had the nerve to insist she comes to our wedding and he will not listen to my protests. Oh, if only Miss Trumble were here!"

For the second time Abigail was attired in her wedding gown. "She is due back this afternoon, just in time for the wedding," said Rachel. "So wicked of Mama to send her away. Do you not wish to eat something?"

"I could not eat anything," said Abigail dismally. "Where is Rupert?"

"He is not supposed to see you until the church," said Rachel. "He received a letter which startled him. He said he had to make a call but would return in time for the wedding."

Lord Burfield had been distressed to receive a letter by hand from an old army friend in which he said he was in great distress over a family matter and begged Lord Burfield to call on him immediately. The army friend lived in Norwood. It took Lord Burfield some time to get there but very little time to find out that he had been tricked. The army friend was in perfect health and spirits and had sent no letter. Lord Burfield was puzzled. But he had still plenty of time to drive back to Park Street, change into his wedding clothes, and get to that church.

Abigail read the letter which had been slipped into her hand by one of the footmen, holding it with shaking hands, blinking her eyes to get those dreadful words back into focus. Purporting to come from "a friend," the letter stated that on that very day, Lord Burfield was entertaining his mistress at Ivy Cottage, Bark Lane, on the far side of the village of Kensington. It was doubtful if he could leave her arms to get to the church.

Then she roused herself from her shocked stupor. She could only think of obeying the instructions of the letter which begged her, for the sake of the good name of her family, not to tell anyone where she was going. She locked her bedroom door, took off her wedding gown, put on a riding dress and then slipped down the backstairs, unobserved.

Outside, Harry waited anxiously for the result of his letter. He had bribed that footman heavily, emphasizing that the letter must be given to Abigail when she was alone. Now all he had to do was to wait and pray that Abigail's jealousy would be enough to drive her from the house without telling anyone.

In a very short time, Abigail erupted from the house in riding dress. Harry smiled to himself as he saw her heading for the mews. He mounted his horse and rode off as fast as the traffic would allow in the direction of Hyde Park toll. He had to get to that cottage before Abigail!

Abigail knew the head groom would never let her take a carriage out again but knew he could hardly refuse her a horse when she said she wished to go riding in the Row.

She felt numb with misery. She would confront the guilty pair and then tell the faithless Lord Burfield that she could never marry him. She blinked back a tear. He probably never meant to turn up at the church at all!

She rode quickly in the direction of Kensington Village and once there asked directions to Bark Lane.

Bark Lane proved to be a narrow country road, a dirt track winding through high hedges. Ivy Lane was an isolated little cottage, shielded by a stand of trees.

Abigail dismounted and tethered her horse to the gate-post. She pushed open the gate. It was a small whitewashed cottage made of daub and wattle, the beams, black with age, criss-crossing the whitewashed walls. The roof was of thatch. The gate screamed on rusty hinges. A flock of rooks rose cawing and wheeling up to the sky. The sun struck down on her back as she walked up the path. A perfect day for a wedding, she thought, fighting back the tears.

She raised her hand to knock at the door and then saw it was open a couple of inches. Rage suffused her. So careless, so unheeding of the conventions, of any decency. She opened the door and walked in. There was a narrow staircase leading to an upper floor. She walked up it. It was then that a feeling of uneasiness began to damp her rage. Empty houses have a certain atmosphere, and she was suddenly sure that no one was in the cottage except herself. The slamming of the front door downstairs made her jump. The wind must have risen, she thought. There were two rooms upstairs, both bedrooms, both empty.

Now dread clutched at her heart. Now she remembered all the people who did not want her to marry Lord Burfield: his parents, Prudence Makepeace, and Mrs. Brochard, to name but a few.

She ran back down the stairs, but the door was securely locked. She ran to the parlour window, noticing for the first time that it, like all the other windows, were barred, and that the bars looked new.

The parlour was sparsely furnished. There was a rickety table in the centre of it and on that table was a letter with her name on it.

She opened it.

*"Dear Miss Beverley,"* she read. *"You are so easily gulled, are you not? So ready to believe the worst. You will stay here until the day of your wedding is over. Then I shall visit you and we*

*shall enjoy ourselves together, shall we not? Harry Devers."*

Harry Devers had ridden back to a rendezvous with Prudence in St. James's Park. "She is safe and sound," he said gleefully. "But the fun is not over yet. You must pen a note saying that Abigail does not want to be married in that wedding gown, as it was so unlucky, and will be waiting for them all at the church."

"They will know it is not Abigail's writing!"

"You say you are sending it for her. No, no, just sign it 'A friend.' "

"They will never believe it. They will get the Runners out!"

"After the fiasco at Mannerling, they will believe anything. Trust me. Ah, you are afraid you will be discovered. Fear not. There is no way they can find out. *I* will never tell anyone."

"But what of you? Abigail will tell everyone it was you."

"She does not know it has anything to do with me," he lied. He had not thought one second beyond revenging himself on Abigail. Prudence took an uneasy little step back. He reeked of brandy. But she had gone this far, and he had said there was no way she could be implicated. She nodded and turned on her heel. She would write that letter.

Lady Beverley was being fanned vigorously and her wrists rubbed. She had swooned after being told that her daughter planned to turn up at the church on her own and not in her wedding gown. Robert Sommerville, Abigail's brother-in-law, who was to have the honour of giving her away, went in search of Miss Trumble, who had just arrived, and held out the letter.

"Fustian!" said Miss Trumble roundly. "Something bad has happened. I do not believe anonymous letters. Oh, Lord Burfield, here's a coil. A letter has arrived supposed to be from a friend of Abigail's to say that she plans not to be married in her wedding gown and will present herself at the church in a dress of her own choice."

"Something very odd is going on," he said, his voice sharp with worry. "I myself received a letter supposed to come from an old army friend who said he was in trouble. I rode there to find out the letter was a lie. Wait here. I will go round to the mews to see if she has taken a carriage out."

It was unfortunate that the distressed Abigail had decided to put up a good front before the groom. "I did point out it was odd to go riding in the Row on the very day of her wedding," said the groom, "but miss just laughed and said mayhap there wouldn't be a wedding to go to."

Lord Burfield clenched his fists in rage. He thought of all Abigail's coldness to him. He thought of how she had tricked Harry Devers. He was suddenly sure it was Abigail who had lured him out to Norwood so that she could make her escape, so that she could then shame him by not turning up.

When this acid view was put to Miss Trumble, she cried out against it, saying Abigail would not do such a thing. But Lord Burfield's parents were there to point out that any young lady who had behaved as Abigail had behaved at Mannerling was mad and devious and had no thought for the conventions.

It was Jessica and Robert Sommerville who finally took charge, stating that the best idea was that everyone should go to the church. Miss Trumble insisted that if Abigail did not appear, then the Runners should be alerted. But she was edgy and worried when Rachel, Lizzie, and Belinda told her of the coldness, interrupted by frequent rows, between Abigail and Lord Burfield. Had Abigail, who had been so overset by Harry Devers, decided that all men were beasts? She gave a superstitious shudder, feeling that she had come back to London with the malign influence of Mannerling sticking to her, infesting her like the plague. For almost the first time in her life, the usually competent Miss Trumble felt helpless.

Abigail looked at the fob-watch pinned to her riding dress. In one hours' time, she was supposed to be marrying Lord Burfield. Everyone would believe she had stood him up. Harry Devers could not possibly let her go free. He would kill her!

She scrubbed her eyes dry. Somehow, some way, she must escape. She tugged at the bars of the windows, but they were immovable. The doors, front and back, were solid. She found a blunt old table knife. She looked up at the low ceiling. She climbed gingerly up on the table and began to chip away at the old plaster on the ceiling between the beams. If she could cut a hole through it and then get up through the thatch, perhaps she could escape that way. But only when she started on her task did she realize how impossible it all was. Bits of plaster rained down on her upturned face. She made another desperate jab with the knife. The table swayed and she fell headlong on the floor. She lay there, winded and bruised and beginning to cry again with sheer fright and despair.

"Oh, God help me!" she cried.

And then she found she was looking at the fireplace.

Prudence Makepeace's lady's-maid was very worried. At first, when Prudence had sent her away so that she could talk privately to Harry Devers, the romantic maid thought it was a love affair and was quite pleased that her rather prim and strict mistress was showing signs of human weakness.

But then Betty reflected, after several meetings had taken place, that her mistress was a great heiress and therefore prey to adventurers, and if Miss Makepeace should run off with this man, she, Betty, would lose her job. When Prudence met Harry for the last time in St. James's Park, Betty as usual walked off out of earshot. She was a pretty girl with glossy black hair and dimpled cheeks and she soon attracted the attentions of two guardsmen.

"Be off with you, sirs," said Betty, but with a giggle. "Whatever will my young mistress say? You will shock her."

"Which is your mistress, my beauty?" asked one of the guardsmen, stroking his magnificently oiled side-whiskers.

"Miss Prudence Makepeace, over there, with that gentleman."

The other guardsman gave a great horse-laugh. "That ain't no gentleman, not by the correct use of the word. That's Harry Devers of Mannerling. If your young mistress consorts with such as he, then she is far from being shocked by anything."

Betty's eyes widened, causing both guardsmen to compliment her on their fineness, but she did not hear a word they said. That, over there, talking to her mistress, was the infamous Harry Devers! For the upper servants heard as much gossip as their betters, and Betty had heard all about Harry.

The distressed maid decided there was nothing else she could do. She would need to report the meetings to Mr. and Mrs. Makepeace.

Abigail rolled over on the floor and stared at the large empty fireplace. It was the ingle-nook kind: two stone seats on either side, iron firedogs, chimney blackened with the smoke of ages. She crawled into the fireplace on her hands and knees and stared upwards, catching her breath as she saw a round of blue sky far above. She raised herself upright inside the chimney-breast and, sending up a little prayer, she scrabbled at the soot-encrusted chimney until her fingers closed on what she had been praying for—climbing rungs for the chimney sweep's boy. It was a miracle they should be there at all, for the cottage was not high enough to warrant them. She seized the first rung and grimly, hauling herself up, began to climb.

Mr. and Mrs. Makepeace were taking tea together. They had just been congratulating themselves on having such a *good* daughter, not at all like that dreadful Abigail Beverley who, of late, had seemed hell-bent on demonstrating to the whole of London society that she did not like her fiancé at all.

"How Burfield can still bring himself to think of marrying the girl," Mrs. Makepeace was saying as Betty walked in, "is quite beyond me. Mrs. Brochard has kept insisting there is still hope. What hope? He will soon be married. What is it, Betty?"

Betty dropped a low curtsy. "I am feared of losing my employ, ma'am," she said with her eyes on the floor. "But I am mortal worried about Miss Makepeace."

"Prudence? Good heavens, what is it? Is she ill?"

"Worse than that, ma'am," said Betty, who was beginning to enjoy herself.

Mrs. Makepeace let out a faint scream. Her husband took her hand and said firmly, "Out with it, girl. If you have something to say, then say it with less Haymarket dramatics."

"Beg pardon, sir. Miss Prudence has been meeting that Harry Devers on the sly."

"You must be mistaken. And if she were, why did you not come to us immediately?"

"Because Miss Prudence would send me packing," said Betty. "Please do not tell her I told you."

"Where have these meetings been taking place?"

"Mostly when she goes out to walk to the shops. In Pall Mall. Places like that. But this morning, it was St. James's Park. Miss Prudence always sends me away so I cannot hear what is being said, but there were two guardsmen in the park and they recognized Mr. Devers. They were flirting with me and I said my mistress would be shocked and they said something to the effect that Miss Prudence could not be shocked by anything if she consorted with such as Mr. Devers."

Mrs. Makepeace's lips trembled. "Send Miss Prudence to us immediately."

"Oh, ma'am," pleaded Betty. "I was only doing my duty. Please don't tell Miss Prudence it was me who told on her or I will lose my job. Don't you see, I could have kept quiet?"

"All right, girl," snapped Mr. Makepeace. "Just fetch Miss Makepeace."

When the maid had left, the couple looked at each other. "There must be some innocent explanation," said Mrs. Makepeace.

Prudence came in, looking, as usual, like a fashion-plate. She was wearing a plain muslin frock of walking length, the front of the bodice and the short sleeves made rather full, the latter gathered with a band and finished with a bow of ribbon. She had not yet removed her bonnet, which was of the cottage shape, the front of straw with a round crown of lavender-blossom silk. A hand-kerchief of the same silk crossed the crown and was tied in a bow under her chin. Under the bon-net was a small cap with a frill of lace. A sash to match the bonnet trimming was tied at the back under a pereline made of three falls of finely crimped muslin. Her long gloves and half-shoes were of buff kid.

She looked a good and modest girl. Mrs. Make-peace surveyed her with a glimmer of hope in her eyes. "Prudence, dear . . ." she began hesitantly, but Mr. Makepeace said angrily, "Why have you been meeting Devers on the sly?"

Prudence turned scarlet and the hope left her mother's eyes.

"I have not been meeting such a man," cried Prudence.

"You have been seen with him when you were sup-posed to be shopping, and only today you were with him in St. James's Park. Out with it!" demanded Mr.

Makepeace. "What were you about? Have you no care for your reputation?"

Prudence did not know what to say. She could not reveal that she had been helping Harry in his plot to capture Abigail Beverley on the day of her wedding.

With a great effort, she put a pious expression on her face. "I knew you would not approve," she said. "I was merely trying to help that poor, unfortunate man."

For the first time in his quiet, orderly life, Mr. Makepeace had a strong desire to hit his daughter.

"That poor, unfortunate man, as you call him, is a notorious lecher."

"He has reformed," said Prudence, casting her eyes modestly down. "He regrets his wicked ways. He sought the company of a good lady like myself."

"Then he should have called here!" howled her exasperated father.

"How could he? You would have refused him admittance."

"I do not know what silly, romantical notions you have been getting into your head," said her father, "but you are not to see him again, and from now on you are confined to the house and you will not go out of it unless accompanied by your parents. Do I make myself clear?"

"Yes, Papa," said Prudence meekly, desperate to escape.

"Go to your room until I have time to discuss this with your mother. You have not heard the last of this!"

Abigail stared upwards in despair. There was that round of blue sky, but it was at the end of a chimney-pot through which she could not possibly get through. She stood on the topmost rung. It bent a little under her feet and gave an ominous creak.

She lunged upwards and struck the side of the chimney-pot with her fist with all her strength. To her amazement, her relief, the old chimney-pot, loosened by centuries of weather, slowly toppled over and fell. She could hear it slithering down the thatch, and then there was a solid thump as it hit the grass in the garden. Sweet fresh air flowed down onto her sooty face. She grasped the edging of the thatch and heaved herself up. She gave a frightened cry as she began to slip back. She thought of Harry Devers, soon to return, and impelled herself up and out with such impetus that she rolled onto the thatch, slid down the roof, with the reeds of the thatch tearing at her gown and at her clutching hands. Her feet struck the lead gutter, which creaked and bent and finally gave. Abigail fell straight down into the garden, and, fortunately for her, onto a pile of soft earth. She stumbled to her feet. Her hands were bleeding, having been cut by the thatch, and she was black with soot from head to foot. She ran to the garden gate. But her horse had gone. Of course Harry would have taken it away. How on earth was she to get to the church?

And then she heard the sound of carriage wheels coming along the road and crouched down behind the hedge, fearful that Harry had returned.

It was supposed to be a small wedding in the church of St. Edmund, King and Martyr in Lombard Street in the City of London. But gossipy society were determined to get a view of this outrageous bride and crowded outside the church, craning their necks, giggling and gossiping. There was an air of holiday, almost like a public hanging. The gingerbread sellers were plying their wares, along with the ballad singers, and there were even street dancers and acrobats to entertain the crowd.

Inside the church, the wedding guests fidgeted and waited. At the altar stood Lord Burfield with an old army friend, Colonel Withers, as his brideman. At the door of the church waited Robert Sommerville with the Beverley sisters.

The Earl of Drezby muttered to his wife, "By Jove, I do believe the bride is not going to come. What a scandal! But our boy has had a lucky escape."

Mrs. Brochard gave a little smile of satisfaction. Rupert had not spoken to her since he told her to leave his house. But now he was seeing for himself what type of family he had been about to ally his name with.

Miss Trumble was worried to death. She hoped that Abigail was simply behaving disgracefully and had run away from her own wedding. For the alternative, that someone had tricked her, that she could be in danger, was almost past bearing. Lady Beverley was very white and for once Miss Trumble felt sorry for her.

The service was supposed to commence at three o'clock. By ten past three, there was a rustling and muttering starting from the guests, which rose louder and louder as everyone began to speculate what had happened to Abigail. Barry, the odd man, seated at the very back of the church, wondered what would happen should it transpire that Abigail had once more shamed a man on his wedding day.

The Beverleys would never rise above this scandal. Where, oh where, was Abigail?

Mr. Tommy Cartwright was not a very happy young man. He was driving his racing curricle slowly along Bark Lane in Kensington and musing sadly on the bitter fact that he had failed to cut a dash in London.

He was nineteen years of age and had come up to Town from the country for his first Season armed with all the requisites necessary to become a dandy. He had a good income, a wardrobe of the first stare, prime horses, membership of White's, got his vouchers of Almack's, and yet he felt friendless and ignored. He had fondly imagined that by the end of the Season he would be dubbed Beau Cartwright, and that the other dandies would be begging him to show them how to tie a cravat. But the men did not crave his company and the beauties of the Season looked at him with indifferent eyes. If only he could have achieved some social success to make them sit up and stare. Everyone was desperate for an invitation to that Beverley girl's wedding. If only he could have secured an invitation! If only . . .

His horse shied and reared and plunged as a black figure darted out in the middle of the road in front of them, waving its arms.

"Whoa!" cried Tommy, reining the horses in. "What the devil . . . ?"

"Oh, please, sir," cried an anguished female voice. "I must get to my wedding."

Thoroughly bewildered, Tommy stared down into a soot-stained face turned up to his.

"I am Abigail Beverley. Please, please, I must get

to the church. Harry Devers locked me up in that cottage so I could not go to my own wedding. Oh, please take me to the City."

Tommy had never been famed for quickness of thought, but he was to remember that as the one moment when his brain worked like lightning. He did not stop to question whether this awful sooty creature was really *the* Abigail Beverley.

"Hop up," he said, "and hang on tight. I'm going to spring 'em. Lombard Street it is."

The noise inside and outside the church was rising to an uproar. Guests had left their pews and were strolling about. The general consensus of opinion was that the disgraceful Abigail Beverley had done it again—she had ruined another wedding. Lizzie, with her other sisters, was crying quietly in the church porch, saying she was sure Abigail would never do such a thing, that something awful had happened to her.

Rachel looked up into Lord Burfield's face with wide, frightened blue eyes as he walked down the aisle to join the little group at the church entrance.

"I think we should all leave here," he said stiffly. "The crowd outside are turning this into a circus and I cannot bear any more."

"*You* cannot bear any more!" cried Rachel furiously. "What about Abigail?"

Animated by worry and anger, she looked heartbreakingly, in that moment, like her twin. Lord Burfield hesitated, but then shook his head. "There is no point in waiting here any longer to provide any more amusement for the gossips. I will make an announcement."

Miss Trumble had joined them. She suddenly

heard loud cheers and laughter from outside, followed by cries of "Make way! Let them through!"

"Wait!" she shouted. "Something has happened."

Lord Burfield strode out of the church.

To loud huzzas, Tommy Cartwright was edging his carriage through the press and beside him sat a soot-stained little figure whom Lord Burfield recognized with a lurch of his heart as Abigail.

He went forward as the carriage pulled up outside the church and held out his arms. Abigail fell down into them, crying, "Harry Devers tricked me. Oh, Rupert, he locked me up in a cottage. Oh, Rupert!"

Lord Burfield drew her into the church. Abigail told her story inside and Tommy, relishing his moment of glory, told his story outside.

"How could you be so easily tricked?" Lord Burfield exclaimed, when Abigail had finished.

"I was jealous," said Abigail, beginning to cry weakly. "You would not explain about Lady Tarrant."

He gathered her in his arms again. "Oh, my darling, how stupid we both have been and how stubborn. We will get you home and arrange the wedding for another day."

"No!" Abigail brushed away the tears, leaving white streaks across her sooty face. "I do not want to wait. Cannot we be married now?"

He gave a sudden laugh. "London will talk about this for days. Yes, my love. We will be married."

"And can someone ask my nice young rescuer to the wedding?"

"I will," said Miss Trumble.

It was the moment of glory that Tommy had always dreamt of. In front of the crowd, he was formally invited to the wedding by Miss Trumble, who also thanked him warmly for being "such a hero."

And so Lord Burfield, with his white satin wedding clothes stained with soot from hugging Abigail, was married to his extremely dirty bride, while two of the male guests went off to fetch the Runners. The hunt was up for Harry Devers.

But Harry had been among the crowd, savouring his "triumph" when, to his horror, he had seen Abigail being driven up to the church. He took to his heels, sweating with fear. He would need to escape before the law caught up with him.

Almost mad with fright when he reached his town house, he shouted to the servants to pack his things and make his travelling-carriage ready. But before the preparations were half done, he heard the roar of an approaching crowd in the street and knew what had happened. The gossip outside the church had spread like wildfire to the mob and the mob were out for his blood.

He ran down to the basement to try to make his way out through the back door, but he retreated quickly as he heard the thud of feet as members of the mob, anticipating that he might try to escape that way, vaulted over the back wall.

Harry scampered back up the stairs, past his terrified servants. Up he went to the attics, into one, climbed on a chair and pushed open the skylight. With luck, he could scramble over the roof and leap to the roof of the adjoining building which, unlike his own, was the start of a terrace, and so across the other roofs to safety. Someone down below saw him and yelled. There was a deep-throated baying from the crowd. Shots came from the end of the street. The militia had arrived.

But Harry was not going to risk waiting for their rescue, for they would arrest him and drag him off in chains to Newgate.

Teetering on the tiles, he ran to the edge of the roof and looked across at the adjoining building. It looked farther away than he had thought.

The splintering of his front door downstairs as the mob burst into his house made up his mind for him. He went back several paces, took a breath, and ran and leaped out into space. But he fell short of the building opposite by a whole foot and plunged downwards towards the stone path which ran between the two houses. He hit the ground with a sickening thud. For a moment, all was blackness, and then the blackness cleared and he was walking into the splendid hall at Mannerling, feeling the house welcoming him back, smelling the Mannerling smell of pot-pourri, beeswax, and wood-smoke. He died with a smile on his lips, the innocent smile of a child.

The gossips had been calling on the Makepeaces all day. First they learned of how Abigail had arrived at the church covered in soot, with her dress torn and her hands bleeding and yet had insisted on getting married there and then.

Prudence commented in a subdued little voice that no doubt Abigail Beverley was worried her groom would escape her, but no, replied the gossips, they were so much in love. Everyone could see that when they left the church together.

Then Prudence learned that Harry had lied to her, that Abigail knew the identity of her captor and that Harry Devers was to be arrested. She turned quite pale. Had Harry told Abigail about *her*? She began to feel quite faint. But then an excited servant burst in with the news that Harry Devers, in an attempt to escape from the mob, had leaped from the roof of his house to his death. Prudence slowly began to feel better. Had Harry talked to Abigail, then the Runners would have called for her by now. She had nothing to fear. But there were more callers, and this time more detailed information. The letter sent to Lord Burfield's home to say that Abigail planned to arrive at the church by herself had been written in a feminine hand, so Harry Devers must have had an accomplice. Prudence became aware of her parents' horrified eyes resting on her. When the last callers had left, Mr. Makepeace said, "You were behind this, Prudence. That is why you were meeting Devers secretly. There is no time now to tell you exactly what I think of you. Speed is of the essence. You must be got out of the country before anyone comes looking for you. No," he added in a fury as Prudence would have spoken, "not another word. We are leaving this night for Naples, leaving like the fugitives we are, but 'fore God, the way I feel at the moment, I would gladly turn you over to the Runners. So make haste and lie me no more lies, or I might change my mind!"

Abigail, in her wedding gown at last, with her train looped over her arm, was waltzing in the arms of her husband. She had resisted all suggestions that she lie down and rest after her ordeal. Abigail felt as if she were floating on air.

Tommy Cartwright was dancing with Rachel, well aware he was the hero of the day. He was saving up every moment to put in a letter home that very night. Two reporters had taken down his story. It would all be in the newspapers on the following morning. The only thing that he regretted was that there were so few guests. He only wished it had been a huge fashionable wedding so that he could have performed on a larger stage. But a large number of society had been outside the church and had witnessed his dramatic arrival. He dreamily ran that magnificent moment of glory through his brain again and trod on Rachel's toes, apologized, and tried to concentrate on his steps.

Lady Evans was there, sitting with Miss Trumble, watching the dancers. "You may have your say, Letitia," said Lady Evans. "But mark my words: money lasts, love don't."

"You still do not think Burfield would have been better off with Prudence Makepeace?"

"Why not? Whatever you may say, that Abigail is a wild one. Can you imagine a real *lady* climbing up a cottage chimney and then insisting on getting wed in all her filth?"

"No," said the governess drily, " a real lady would have waited patiently for Harry Devers to come back and rape her. Furthermore, to my way of thinking, little Miss Prudence was involved in this in some way."

"Pooh, how could she be?" demanded Lady Evans. "She doesn't even know Devers, and her family would not have let him near her."

Barry came into the saloon in Lord Burfield's house, where the dancing was being held, and made his way round the room until he reached Miss Trumble.

"Oh, miss," he said, "the most shocking thing. Several people have come forward to say as how they saw that Miss Prudence Makepeace talking to Mr. Harry Devers in the street on several occasions, and only this morning two guards officers saw them in St. James's Park."

Miss Trumble swung round and said to Lady Evans, "So what do you think of your precious Prudence now?"

"I cannot believe it," cried old Lady Evans, her lips trembling. "But if she is guilty, she will be arrested. What a scandal! Scandal upon scandal!"

"Let us not spoil the festivities with any more dramas," said Miss Trumble. "Come, Barry, we will go to the Makepeaces and see what we can find out."

They took a hack to the Makepeaces' town house. A butler answered the door and said stonily that the family were not at home. Miss Trumble fished in her capacious reticule and extracted a guinea and held it up. "Really not at home?" she asked sweetly. "I am a friend of Lady Evans."

The butler leaned forward and looked up and down the street and then said with a little jerk of his head, "Step inside."

She and Barry walked into the hall. The butler held out one plump white hand. Miss Tremble put the guinea into it, which the butler first bit to see if it was real, and then slipped it into his pocket.

"They've gone to Italy. All in a rush, like. Usually it takes the quality weeks to prepare for such a journey to foreign parts." Miss Tremble felt quite weak with relief. She had realized that if Prudence Makepeace had been arrested, the scandal would have quite destroyed her old friend, Lady Evans. What a tale of revenge and jealousy it had all been!

# Chapter Seven

*To marry is to domesticate the Recording
Angel. Once you are married, there is
nothing left for you, not even suicide, but
to be good.*

—ROBERT LOUIS STEVENSON

LORD BURFIELD BEGAN to think that his bride
meant to dance the whole of the night away. And
because Abigail continued to dance, so the guests
continued as well. Lady Beverley had recovered
from all the shocks and alarms and finally woken to
the fact—prompted, of course, by Miss Trumble—
that she now had three daughters who had all married well.

Miss Trumble, who had returned to report to Lady
Evans about the flight of the Makepeaces, watched
anxiously as the festivities continued. There were
violet shadows under Abigail's eyes. The girl was
obviously tired after all the strain of her imprison-
ment and escape.

Miss Trumble gave a little click of impatience.
Unless Abigail made a move to "behave like a proper
wife"—as Miss Trumble delicately put it to herself—this marriage might end its first day with a
monumental row. Abigail was dancing with Mr. Cartwright, so Miss Trumble rose and approached Lord
Burfield, who was helping himself to another glass of
champagne.

"To put it bluntly, my lord," said Miss Trumble, "is it not time you retired?"

A flicker of amusement shone in his blue eyes. "It is indeed. But alas, my young bride appears to be enjoying the company of others too much."

"Bride nerves," said the governess. "And unless you make a move, they are going to get worse."

He gave a reluctant laugh. "My Abigail has been through so much, I do not want anything more to trouble her this day."

"Some things have to be resolved on the spot."

The dance was finished. Abigail was curtsying to Tommy. Lord Burfield crossed to her side.

"It is time we retired, my sweeting." He saw fear dart through her eyes and fought down a surge of impatience. Was she stupid enough to think him another Harry Devers? And then it dawned on him that to take her upstairs for their first night as man and wife under the same roof as the guests, where some of the men were drunkenly beginning to make lewd remarks, would not help. "Go to your room," he said, "and put on your carriage gown."

"Where are we going?"

"I'll think of somewhere. Now, go!"

Abigail went up to her room, where she was soon joined by her sisters. "Where are you going?" asked Lizzie. "I thought you were staying here!"

"Lord Burfield, I mean Rupert, has suddenly decided to take me somewhere, I don't know where," said Abigail, her voice muffled as Betty lifted the wedding gown over her head.

"I think it is all very romantic," sighed Rachel. She stroked the folds of the wedding gown. "How beautiful this is. I wonder if I shall ever wear a wedding gown."

"You are bound to." Lizzie peered in the mirror and tugged at a strand of her red hair. "Why was I ever cursed with red hair? How can one ever be classed as a beauty with red hair? Do you know, it is said the Duke of Wellington shaved his son's eyebrows because they were red?"

"Miss Trumble says it is because of the prejudice against the Scottish people," said Belinda. "I have never met one Scottish person with red hair. But people will have it they are all red-haired."

"What do you think will happen to Mannerling now?" asked Lizzie. "I mean, I doubt very much if the Deverses will continue to live there."

"I do not care," said Abigail. "The very thought of the place frightens me now. I think it tricks us all, offering peace and tranquillity and supplying instead obsession and danger and shame. I never want to see it again. Do you ... Lizzie? *Lizzie?*"

"No, of course not," said Lizzie hurriedly, too hurriedly, thought Jessica worriedly, remembering her own terrible obsession with the place, which had nearly lost her the love of Robert Sommerville, now her husband.

"I wonder if we shall ever see Isabella again," she went on. "But we all seem to wed so hurriedly that there is never time for her to make arrangements to come over from Ireland. But all her letters are so happy. I hope you will be as happy as I am and as Isabella is, Abigail."

Abigail longed to ask this elder married sister about the mysteries of the marriage bed, but in an age when young misses were not even supposed to mention dreadful words like "legs," she found she could not bring herself to say anything.

They all helped the maid to prepare her for this unknown journey. Lizzie began to become tearful. One after one, her sisters were leaving home, and soon she would be left alone.

Lady Beverley came in and aimed a kiss somewhere in the air above Abigail's cheek. "Be good, my child," she said sententiously, "and obey your husband in all matters. Ah, if only your dear papa could have been alive this day."

A guilty silence fell on her daughters. The late Sir William Beverley had become a shadowy figure in their minds. They had all been so bitter about the loss of Mannerling, had blamed him for that loss, that they had not mourned his passing very much.

"You must remember, Abigail, to tell your husband his duty towards the impoverished Beverleys," said Lady Beverley.

Abigail surveyed her mother with cynical eyes. "You mean, I am to ask him to send you money?"

"You were always too blunt, my child. Remind him of his duty."

"He has no duty to you," said Abigail with a flash of anger.

Miss Trumble entered the room and said quietly. "Are you ready, Abigail? Lord Burfield is waiting for you."

The sisters crowded around Abigail, hugging her and kissing her. Then, as she was leaving the room, Abigail kissed Miss Trumble on the cheek and whispered, "Keep them safe from Mannerling."

Then, followed by them all, Abigail went downstairs

to where the guests were gathered around Lord Burfield's travelling-carriage. Her hurriedly packed trunks were brought down by the footmen and put in the rumble. Lord Burfield was driving himself. He leaned over from the box and held out his hand. "Come and join me."

Abigail grasped his hand and was lifted up. The carriage began to move slowly away. "Goodbye," called Abigail's sisters, clustered around Miss Trumble.

Tommy Cartwright, overcome by fame and champagne, began to cry noisily, and that started everyone else off. The sound of sobs died away in the distance as the carriage turned the corner of the street.

To Abigail's relief, her husband did not talk, merely drove his team competently along the Great West Road, the wheels sending up spurts of gravel. The countryside swam in the golden evening light. Abigail's eyes began to close. She leaned her head against Lord Burfield's shoulder and fell asleep.

I wonder if she realizes how nervous *I* am about this night ahead, he thought ruefully. Unlike my peers, I do not find the idea of bedding a virgin exciting. What a responsibility, particularly after all she has been through.

Abigail awoke as the carriage rolled under the arch of a posting-house in Richmond. Underneath them the carriage door opened and Barry emerged and ran into the posting-house. He returned after a few minutes, followed by the landlord.

"A room has been prepared for you, my lord," said Barry.

"Why Barry?" asked Abigail, sleepily as he lifted her down from the box. "He is not one of your servants."

"I thought you would be more comfortable with a familiar face. This is the one time in our life when we do not wish to be surrounded by servants."

Abigail stifled a giggle as a whole retinue of servants rushed from the inn to bow and scrape and carry their bags.

They followed the landlord upstairs. He threw open the door of a bedchamber. There was a great four-poster bed, its curtains looped back. The casement windows were open to show a vista of the slowly moving river.

Maids appeared to unpack their bags. Abigail rested her elbows on the window-sill and watched the river turning gold in the setting sun.

And then she heard the door close quietly. The servants had left. She straightened up and gripped the window-sill with nervous fingers. He would surely leave her to wash and undress and so delay that terrifying moment when she would face the unknown.

He came up behind her and put his hands on her shoulders. "I am very frightened I will hurt you, my love, or give you a disgust of me. And you are frightened as well, are you not? Let us be frightened together."

He turned her round to face him and then kissed her gently on each cheek and then softly on her mouth. For a long time all she felt was his lips moving against her own, his body pressed against her, and all she heard was the sleepy bedtime chatter of the birds outside the window and the soft lapping of the water. Her lips began to move against his own in response and she buried her hands in his thick fair hair. How she had fretted over that terrible embarrassment of undressing! And yet, as his hands began to move over her body, unfastening the long row of buttons at the front of her gown, loosening the tapes at the back, it all felt so natural. And when she was finally lying naked in his arms, she lost her virginity in such a surge of red passion that she barely noticed the pain, writhing under his busy body and moaning against him.

She awoke at dawn and lay and stretched. She heard a noise from outside and climbed stiffly from the high bed, pulled on a wrapper and went to the still-open window and looked down. Barry was standing directly below the window on a strand of shingle, throwing stones into the river like a schoolboy. As if conscious of her gaze, he turned and looked up. Abigail's radiant face looked down at him.

"Happy, miss?" he called up softly.

"Oh, yes, Barry, so happy."

He bowed and moved quickly away.

Abigail climbed back into bed, and leaning on one elbow, studied her lord's face and then tenderly brushed a lock of hair back from his forehead. He awoke and pulled her across his chest. "Where were we?" he murmured.

Miss Trumble awoke with a scratching at the door. "Come," she called sleepily. She looked at the clock on the mantel. Nine o'clock. She had slept later than usual because, no matter how late she stayed up the night before, the governess usually awoke early.

Barry came in, a sheepish smile on his face.

She sat up and exclaimed, "Barry! What are you doing here? You are supposed to be with them."

"They are at Richmond and they will not miss me. I hired a horse on Lord Burfield's account and rode straight here to tell you all is well."

"Now how can you know that, Barry?"

"I was down at the river as the sun came up, and I was below their bedroom window. I looked up and there was Miss Abigail, I mean Lady Burfield. I asked her if she was happy and she said yes, she was, and she looked so beautiful."

"And you rode straight to tell me. How good of you, Barry. How very good. Three gone and three more to go. Surely we cannot expect more success."

"We'll see, miss. Will you be staying on? It is not as if you need to."

"On the contrary. I need the employment very much."

Barry looked at her shrewdly. "But not for the money, I reckon."

"Really, Barry, what odd ideas you do have. I am an impoverished governess," said Miss Trumble severely, settling her night-cap of fine old Brussels lace more firmly on her head.

Barry grinned ruefully and bowed and left. There was some mystery about Miss Trumble, but whatever it was, she was certainly not going to tell him.

Rachel, Belinda, and Lizzie were gathered in Rachel's bedroom that morning. "We are staying here for two more weeks," said Rachel. "I think it is decidedly odd to stay on in Lord Burfield's house when he is not here, but you know Mama, she is counting the saving on food and candles. I feel empty without Abigail, and yet I feel she is very happy."

"What will happen to us now?" asked Lizzie in a small voice. "We will soon go back to the country and we cannot expect to find handsome gentlemen falling for us."

"I feel as long as we have our Miss Trumble, then things will happen to us," said Rachel.

"Miss Trumble cannot do everything. She did not conjure up Lord Burfield for Abigail or make him fall in love with her," pointed out Belinda.

"But she mysteriously organized invitations for us," said Rachel. "Did you hear that Prudence Makepeace was behind the plot to make Abigail miss her wedding, and she has escaped the law? Her parents have taken her abroad. They fled last night. Miss Trumble said she was relieved because a court case would have meant a dreadful scandal."

Lizzie gave a little shiver. "I hope she never comes back to England. Think of the malice behind her actions. I assume it was she who wrote that letter?"

Rachel nodded.

Belinda said, "I, for one, am never going to think of Mannerling again. Isabella, Jessica, and Abigail need never have suffered anything at all had they let go of that dreadful place. It was our home and we loved it, and yet everything to do with the house brings misery."

"It's only a house," said Rachel. "It's our obsession with the place that has caused all the trouble. We have all earned a bad reputation because of it. I was dancing at a ball with an attractive young man, Sir Peregrine Darcy. He was very charming and he seemed pleased with my company. He took me in for supper and soon we were chatting away like old friends. Then he suddenly looked at me and exclaimed, 'Beverley! Of course! I knew I had heard that name.' He grew very guarded and rather remote and soon he turned to speak to the lady on his other side and did not turn back to me. It was all very lowering." She added in low voice, "Perhaps we will never marry now."

"Spinsters!" said Lizzie in hollow tones. "Spinsters all. The Beverley spinsters."

They looked at each other and then Belinda said bracingly, "Miss Trumble will think of something. She always does."

But she looked as if she did not believe what she had just said.

Harry Devers was buried at Mannerling. There was a private chapel not far from the house. It had not been used by Sir William or Lady Beverley or Mr. and Mrs. Devers, who preferred to attend the village church. But it had a small quiet graveyard, full of the Beverley ancestors. The chapel was opened for the funeral and Mr. Stoddart, the vicar, conducted the service.

Mrs. Devers, supported by her husband, stood by the graveside, hearing the words of the burial service tolling in her head.

" 'The days of our age are threescore years and ten; and though men be so strong, that they come to fourscore years: yet is their strength then but labour and sorrow; so soon passeth it away, and we are gone.

" 'But who regardeth the power of thy wrath: for even thereafter as man feareth, so is thy displeasure.' "

Had God been displeased with Harry? wondered Mrs. Devers. She was past crying, and was in a state of half-numb bewilderment. A dank drizzle was falling from a leaden sky. A willow tree had been planted beside the grave, a whole willow tree, specially put there for the sad occasion. Water dripped from its leaves onto the coffin.

Memories of Harry flitted through Mrs. Devers's brain—Harry as a child, smashing his toys, Harry punching his tutor, Harry getting that maidservant pregnant, the girl crying rape and having to be paid to keep silent. And now Harry was gone, and with him all the worry and trouble and turmoil. Harry was quiet at last and buried near the home he had stayed in for such a short time and which he had loved so much.

Mr. Devers had bought a handsome house by the sea at Brighton. There would be fresh breezes, fashionable company, and a whole change of life, away from Mannerling and all its unhappy memories. Mrs. Devers found her mind was slipping away from her dead son towards the pleasures of this change of scene and she felt guilty.

Prudence Makepeace stood on the deck of the *Bella Ann* as the ship sailed through the blue waters of the Mediterranean bound for Naples. She had put all the scandal behind her, would not even think about it. Nothing, after all, had been her fault, as she had told her parents over and over again. Harry had meant to play a little joke on the Beverleys, that she had believed. She would not have *dreamt* of going through with it had she known he had any deep plot in mind.

She was uneasily aware that, for the first time in

their well-ordered lives, her parents no longer believed a word she said. She gave a little shrug. There was a handsome officer on board who was much taken with her, and that had done much to restore her *amour propre*. She would make a dazzling marriage in Naples, so dazzling that London society would soon forget about her little trouble and welcome her back. She would cut the Beverleys, of course. She drifted off into a dream of arriving at Almack's on the arm of some Italian prince. The Beverley sisters would be there, the three unwed ones. In her mind's eye, they had grown old and withered, and they looked at her with hungry, envious eyes, jealous of her good fortune.

Abigail and her husband had been travelling from posting-house to posting-house wrapped up in love, lost in each other, until at last, when they were having breakfast one morning, Lord Burfield said, "I think it is time we returned to London. With any luck, your family will have left for the country."

"Why do you say that in just that tone of voice, my love?" asked Abigail, her blue eyes narrowing. "I was looking forward to seeing them."

"To be frank," he said, "I am not looking forward to meeting your mama again. She must be the most unnatural and mercenary mother it has been my ill-luck to come across."

The fact that this was exactly what Abigail herself thought of her mother did not stop her temper from flaring.

"How can you be so unkind?" she cried. "Yes,

Mama does count the pennies, but she has had much to bear since Papa died."

"Many people have much to bear in this life. It's Clarence House to a Charlie's shelter that she has asked you to ask me to send her money."

"She never did!" lied Abigail, her face turning red with mortification. "Why are you jeering at me in that horrible way?"

He smiled. "There! I am sorry. But my anger against your mother is on your behalf. Had you been better brought up, you would not have concocted that silly plot to wed Harry Devers."

"I was trying to save Rachel, you . . . you pompous fool!" shouted Abigail.

"Do control yourself," said her husband evenly and buttered a piece of toast.

"You are horrid, horrid and I *hate* you! I am going out for some fresh air."

"Don't slam the door after you." The crash of the door as Abigail departed drowned out his words.

Now as cold with anger as she had been hot, Abigail went up to their room and changed into a walking dress and half-boots, put on a bonnet, and then went back downstairs and out of the inn and through the bustle of the yard.

Two young misses were descending from a carriage. I should warn them about marriage, thought Abigail tearfully. I have married a monster!

She walked into the market town, suddenly wishing she could go home and join her sisters and forget she had ever been married. They would play battledore and shuttlecock in the garden and then gather in the cosy parlour in the evening and sew and read. She missed her twin.

Stall-holders and entertainers were busy in the

main square, setting up for a fair. Momentarily diverted, she watched the arrangements and then walked on through the town and so out the other side. Walking was soothing her. The early morning mist was beginning to burn off the fields and all the countryside appeared to be coming to life.

It had been raining heavily the day before, and the deep ruts and holes in the road gleamed with water.

She heard some vehicle approaching and drew to the side of the road. A curricle driven by some local country buck came hurtling around the corner. As the carriage passed Abigail it went straight through a puddle and sent a wave of muddy water up over her before disappearing around a bend.

Abigail cried out in dismay. She was soaked with muddy water from head to foot.

"There, now," said a woman's voice from behind her. "Them young bucks pay no heed to nothing or no one."

Abigail swung round, scrubbing at her muddy face with an ineffectual wisp of handkerchief. A stout countrywoman was leaning over the garden gate of her cottage, surveying Abigail with concern. "You'd best step inside and I'll dry you off, miss," she said. "Come along. You can't go walking about in that state."

Abigail meekly followed her in to a country parlour which doubled as a kitchen. "You just go to the fire and get out of those clothes. I'm Mrs. Plumb."

Abigail held out her hand. "Lady Burfield," she said shyly.

"A lady! And you walking the roads without so much as a maid. Dearie me. Well, let's clean you up, my lady. There's no one here but me. My husband and son are out in the fields. I'll get you something to put on."

Abigail took off her bonnet and carriage dress and was standing by the fire in her shift when Mrs. Plumb returned with a patchwork quilt which she wrapped around Abigail. Then she swung the kettle on the idlejack over the fire. "I do rough cleaning twice a week for squire's lady," said Mrs. Plumb, "and her gave me a twist of tea."

"Oh, you must not waste it on me," said Abigail, knowing that the tea was probably being saved for an occasion.

"I'll be able to tell everyone how I entertained a real lady, so t'won't be wasted. Now sit down in that chair and keep warm." She picked up Abigail's muddy clothes and bustled off. After some time, she came back, lifted the now boiling kettle off the fire and proceeded to make a pot of tea, shaking the leaves into the pot from a little twist of tissue paper.

"Now what was you doing of, walking on your own like that, my lady?"

The desire to confide in someone was too much for Abigail. "I am newly wed, on my honeymoon," she said. "I had a row with my husband." And she burst into tears.

"There, now. Mercy me. Did he beat you?"

"No, no, nothing like that," said Abigail, scrubbing at her tears with a corner of the quilt. "He criticized my mother."

"Oh, you'll need to get used to things like that, my

lady. They never likes the mother-in-law. Did he have reason?"

"He said she was a miser."

"That be cruel. Not as if it's true, now is it?"

"Well, as a matter of fact, it is. I think ... I think I grew angry because I owe him so much. I had little dowry to offer and had created such a scandal that I thought no one would want to marry me."

"I tell you, my lady, gratitude do cause a mort of rows. But you must get used to rows. They're part and parcel of marriage."

"But he said he loved me," wailed Abigail. "He should not be nasty to me if he loves me."

"Oh, well, it is a pity they're human just like us. I tell you, if your good lord don't know where you are, he'll be worried sick. The sun's hot now and I sponged down your gown and hung it over the bushes. 'Twill be dry in a trice. I can't do anything about your bonnet. You finish your tea and get dressed again and I'll walk you back. Where are you staying?"

"The Eagle."

"That's where we'll go and as fast as possible."

Abigail, as she hurriedly dressed, was beginning to become alarmed. What if Rupert had decided he had made a mistake and had gone off and left her? From hating him and wishing she had never married him, she was now back in love, and more deeply than before.

When she left the cottage with Mrs. Plumb, she was hard put not to take to her heels and run. Mrs. Plumb, a plump, comfortable sort of woman, walked with a slow, rolling gait. Abigail was increasingly alarmed to find out how far she had walked from the town. As they approached it, the noise of the fair reached their ears.

And then, with a lurch of her heart, Abigail saw Lord Burfield striding out along the road towards her, his face grim. She flew towards him and straight into his arms, crying, "Oh, Rupert, I am so sorry . . . so sorry."

"You minx," he said, giving her a little shake. "You frightened me to death."

Abigail told him breathlessly of the carriage which had soaked her and of Mrs. Plumb's kindness, ending with, "And I drank her precious tea and I know she must have been saving it for something special."

"Mrs. Plumb can have a whole case of the finest tea," he said, holding her close. He bent his head and kissed her passionately. Mrs. Plumb heaved a romantic sigh and turned and walked back home. She knew they had forgotten her very existence. But she was to learn that such forgetting was only temporary when a whole tea chest of tea was delivered to her the following day, along with what seemed to her dazzled eyes like a two-years' supply of groceries, with goods such as white flour, sugar, salted hams, and every imaginable delicacy.

Barry was pleased to see them return together and disappear up to their room. He was even more pleased to learn later that they were to return to London, which meant he could leave for the country.

"We will never, ever quarrel again, Rupert," said Abigail passionately as she lay in his arms that night.

"No, never," he agreed.

But of course they did, for they were very much in love.

The Beverleys were finally settled back at Brookfield House, along with Barry and Miss Trumble. Mannerling, they learned, stood empty, apart from a caretaker and his wife, awaiting its next owner.

For some reason she could not explain to herself, Miss Trumble drove herself over to Mannerling one day. As the little Beverley carriage rolled up the drive, the house lay before her, gracious and elegant in the sunlight.

"Whoa!" she said to the horse, stopping the carriage in front of the main door. The door was standing open and there were faint sounds from the kitchens, showing the whereabouts of the caretaker and his wife.

Miss Trumble walked into the great hall. Sunlight was filtering through the cupola above the staircase and sending rainbow prisms of light down from the great chandelier.

The governess looked about her. "Nothing to worry about," she said aloud. "Nothing more than a great pile of bricks and plaster."

A sudden gust of wind blew the great main door shut behind her. Above her the chandelier began to revolve slowly, the crystals sending down an eerie tinkling sound.

Miss Trumble was suddenly aware of an almost tangible feeling of menace. She ran to the door and twisted the handle and tugged at it furiously, suddenly terrified that she had been locked in by supernatural forces. But the door suddenly swung open and she was free and out in the sunlight.

I am become fanciful in my old age, the governess chided herself as she drove off.

But she could not help noticing that the day was still and warm, with hardly a breath of air. Certainly no wind. No wind at all. . . .